THE GOSSIP

NEW WAVE NEWSROOM

JENNY HOLIDAY

new wave
newsroom

Edited by Gwen Hayes. Copyedited by Polly Watson. Cover design and formatting by Zack Taylor. Cover photo by lj1980s via Deposit Photos.

First edition October 4, 2016

ISBN 978-0-9950927-2-3

For ZT.

CHAPTER ONE

September 1980

DAWN

It wasn't like I was actually doing anything wrong. I was just *standing* there. Is it my fault that "there" happened to be the parking lot of the strip mall that was home to Allenhurst Discount Liquors? The last time I checked, it was a free country. I'm allowed to stand in a parking lot. And anyway, how did the campus cop who came swooping in like he was Clint Eastwood escaping from Alcatraz know that I wasn't standing there killing time until my appointment for a fitting at Hearing Aid Depot? Or contemplating a purchase at Billy's Bait and Tackle?

"Because these guys walked out of the liquor store and made their way directly to you, whereupon I observed them hand you a brown paper bag. Then I observed you hand them a wad of cash," said the hulking cop, who was apparently intent on ruining my Alpha Phi rush week assignment, which was to procure six bottles of vodka for tonight's party at Delta Chi, Alpha Phi's brother frat.

I had to get into Alpha Phi. *Had* to. This wasn't high school. If I wanted to be at the top of the social pyramid at Allenhurst College, being an Alpha Phi sister was a sure-fire shortcut. And let's face it, if I wasn't popular, I wasn't anything. I wasn't too proud to admit that to myself. My looks were only okay, though I could rock some bitchin' bangs and was known for my elaborate, multicolored eye shadow designs. I wasn't hugely smart—I only got into Allenhurst College because my father went here and he donates buckets of money to them. So popularity was what I had to work with.

I had done a ton of research the summer before coming here and had decided that Alpha Phi was my ticket to social status. I wasn't even looking to get a bid anywhere else and had focused all my rush week efforts on impressing the sisters. I had already done all the sisters' eye makeup for tonight—and there were *fifty-two* of them. That was a lot of effort already invested, so I'd be damned if Officer Unfriendly here was going to tank my chances.

I sized him up, trying to figure out how to play this. He was looking at my driver's license while the two Delta Chi juniors I'd sweet-talked into buying for me produced theirs for another officer. My officer was built, I'll say that much about him—much more so than the one dealing with the guys. Muscular arms strained against his blue button-down cop shirt like they could barely be contained. A trim waist topped off a pair of legs encased in navy blue cargo pants tucked into a pair of black combat boots. He had close-cropped dark hair, and he was frown-ing. He reminded me a little of a younger Erik Estrada from *CHiPS*, except Officer Ponch was always smiling, whereas this guy looked like he was sucking on a Sour Patch Kid. It was hard to really get a read on him, though, because a pair of mirrored aviator sunglasses obscured his eyes.

I made an exaggerated sniff, which drew his attention. "Officer"—I glanced at his name tag—"Perez, I'm really sorry." I put on my best puppy-dog face. "I guess I got carried away with the idea of being in college. It's the end of the first week of classes, you know, and I was feeling a little homesick, so a few of us were going to have a little get-together."

"A little get-together?" His tone was incredulous, and I could imagine him raising his eyebrows behind those glasses even though I couldn't see it happening. When I didn't answer right away, he said, "You're buying for the Delta Chi party tonight. That isn't a 'little gathering.'"

"I am not! I—"

"Forget it, Dawn," said one of the frat guys. "Officer Perez knows everything about Allenhurst College. There's no escaping him once you're in his clutches."

I shivered a little at that notion but shook it off. Well, okay, maybe I wasn't getting that vodka, but that didn't mean I couldn't manage the fallout from the situation. Because Officer Perez was starting to look like maybe he wasn't going to be satisfied with merely issuing a warning.

I manufactured a louder sniff. This one drew everyone's attention: the two frat guys, Officer Perez, and his partner all turned to me. I noted that Officer Unfriendly and his sidekick were wearing different uniforms, a fact I filed away for later. Right now, I had to follow up on that sniff.

"You aren't going to call my parents, are you?" Never mind that I only had one, and that Daddy finding out I was drinking probably wouldn't even rate a phone call. I stuck out my lower lip and tried to make it quiver, not enough that I could be accused of purposeful manipulation, but enough—I hoped—that I was communicating some remorse.

"Nope," said Officer Perez, totally unaffected by my emotional display. "You're eighteen. Welcome to adulthood."

"Welcome to adulthood, yet I'm not allowed to buy alcohol?"

"That is correct." He handed my ID to the cop next to him, and that cop flipped open a little notepad and started writing on it.

"You're a campus cop," I said, letting my gaze rake over Perez's belt. It held a baton and handcuffs and a few other things I didn't recognize, but no gun. The other guy had a gun. And there was the difference in the uniforms I'd noticed earlier.

He glanced at the patch on his right biceps that read ALLENHURST COLLEGE PD. It was stretched taut over the muscle. "And you have a talent for stating the obvious."

"Do you even have jurisdiction here? Because we're not actually on campus." We were a mere two blocks from it, but still. If he wasn't going to respond to my remorseful-little-girl act, maybe I could wiggle out through a procedural loophole.

"That's why this guy"—he jerked his thumb at the colleague I'd come to think of as Good Cop—"is writing your ticket."

"Teamwork," Good Cop said, smiling as he ripped off the ticket and held it out to me. "Allenhurst PD at your service, miss."

"Oh, so you need a real cop to close your deals." I was

being a brat now, but I hated the fact that this big guy, this big *gunless* guy, could just step in and ruin everything.

The big gunless guy in question took a step toward me. God, he *was* big. Maybe he didn't need a gun because of those tree-trunk arms. They looked like they were more than sufficient to take on any villain. "Perhaps you'd prefer that instead of issuing you that fifty-dollar possession ticket, I have my 'real cop' friend here arrest you," he said. "And hey, while we're at it, we'll get your friends for furnishing alcohol to a minor."

"You can't do that!"

He took another step, leaving only a few inches between us. My eyes were level with the middle of his chest, so I had to crank my neck back to maintain eye contact. He was probably doing it on purpose, trying to intimidate me and compensate for his lack of a gun.

He smirked. "Perhaps you'd care to add resisting arrest?"

Ugh! What a dickweed! The last thing I needed was to get the Delta Chi guys in trouble. That would hurt my Alpha Phi chances more than anything. So I took a step back—grudgingly. "No…sir."

I wasn't sure why I added the "sir," but something flared in his eyes when I said it, and he took the ticket from the other cop and held it out. I extended my hand, and instead of letting go of the paper once I had hold of it, he pressed it into my palm and used his hand to close my fingers over it. Then he used his other hand to cradle mine, which resulted in him holding my closed fist between his hands like it was the filling in a hand sandwich. It was the kind of gesture you'd make if you were giving someone something really important, like a lost heirloom or, I don't know, the keys to the kingdom. Not a ticket for underage drinking.

His hands were—of course—huge. They engulfed my fist. It occurred to me, with a jolt, that these were the hands of a man. I'd had boyfriends in high school, but looking at Officer Unfriendly's behemoth chest and feeling his warm, callused hands totally surrounding mine made me feel like the emphasis with past boyfriends had been on the *boy* part.

I'd been unknowingly holding my breath, which was stupid, because when I remedied that fact, the resultant inhale came out sounding perilously close to a gasp. Officer Unfriendly dropped my hands and pressed his lips together as if the stick up his ass were being shoved even higher. "Welcome to college, Miss Hathaway."

CHAPTER TWO

December 1980

ARTURO

It was amusing the way everyone at Allenhurst College thought I was some kind of all-knowing seer, ruling campus from my omniscient post on high. These kids were so melodramatic. At twenty-eight, I wasn't that much older than some of them, but there was a gulf between us that had to do with more than chronological age.

I didn't have any sixth-sense knowledge telling me that tonight was Delta Chi's big holiday party. After six years on campus, I knew the place. It didn't take a genius to figure out that when you broke up a raging kegger on the last Friday of exam period at the same frat house for the second year in a row, perhaps there was an underlying pattern at work. And when you added in years three through six, you could be pretty damn sure that tonight's dose of trouble was going to have Delta Chi's name all over it.

"How do you always *know*, man?" said Royce Waldorf, the shirtless, Santa-hat-wearing junior who opened the door when I pounded on it. Further examination revealed that not only was Royce shirtless, he was wearing a bedsheet around his waist. Perfect. A Christmas toga party. That *was* a new twist. "Who narced?"

"Aren't you going to invite me in?" I asked, not waiting for Royce to answer as I pushed my way into the frat's foyer, which was clogged with coats and dotted with puddles I hoped were from snow that had melted off the mountain of boots piled against the door. Because I had the spirit of Christmas in my heart, I refrained from pointing out that they were a fire hazard.

"Please come in, *amigo*," Royce said sneeringly as he closed the door behind us. The kid was trouble. In addition to being a snob and a racist, he'd had more than his share of citations: underage drinking, marijuana possession, driving under the influence. But since his father was Massachusetts senator Nick Waldorf, magically, nothing ever stuck to him. I couldn't wait for the punk to graduate and move on. But, I reminded myself, I would be gone from Allenhurst College before Royce was. In fact, if I kept to what I'd told Dad last week, this would be my last Alpha Phi holiday party. If I felt a hint of regret at that notion, I shoved it away.

"We were being quiet. God*damn* it. How do you always *know*?"

I merely raised my eyebrows and moved past him, threading my way through a hot, stinky pit of young bodies. I cursed myself for forgetting my earplugs, not so much because the music was loud—I could deal with loud —but because it was Dan Fogelberg. I was more of a Miles

Davis guy myself. Besides, what kind of self-respecting frat played Dan Fogelberg?

"Most of these people are legal, man," Royce said, trailing me as if I were giving a house tour.

I stopped and turned. "First thing? It's not *man*. It's not *amigo*. It's *officer*." Royce's nose wrinkled in distaste, but I didn't give a shit. "Second thing: If you had the IQ of this sofa"—I patted the ripped, grungy monstrosity in front of me, on which a guy and a girl were going at it like it was their last night on Earth, totally oblivious to the fact that the fuzz had arrived—"you would realize that by telling me that 'most' of these people are legal, you're admitting that some of them aren't."

I wasn't trying to be a dick. I wasn't one of those cops who was in it for the power. The small police force at Allenhurst College was granted its authority through the police services board in the surrounding city of Allenhurst, and we shared their motto: Protection, Service, Community. I believed in that shit. Allenhurst was small—it was no Boston, as my father and other assorted Beantown relatives were forever reminding me, but until I decided to make the much-anticipated move to the city force, I was and would remain utterly loyal to Allenhurst College. The school was known for attracting rich white kids who weren't smart enough for the Ivies. Their lives were nothing like my own had been, but I cared about those rich white kids. It was my job to care about them.

Which sometimes meant saving them from themselves.

I saw her across the room. I'm not sure why I was surprised. Dawn Hathaway, though she was only halfway through her freshman year, was on her way to becoming the queen bee of this campus. Where else would I expect her to be on a Friday night at the end of the term? The library? The people around me were giving me a wide berth. They didn't know that I didn't generally go into parties like this gunning for conflict. My MO was to let the people who were capable of it scurry off and then make sure the non-scurriers were going to be okay. I usually had to make an example of a few of the most blatant lawbreakers, but I wasn't in the mood tonight. It was almost Christmas. Once the semester officially finished, our force's workload would plummet, and I was looking forward to a long stretch at my parents' place in South Boston. Well, I could do without my dad constantly riding my ass about my "glorified security guard" gig, but my mom's Christmas spread was not to be missed, and one of my sisters had a new baby I had yet to meet.

But, yeah, this crowd didn't know that I was feeling all "goodwill toward men" and shit, so they were clearing out pretty fast, which suited me fine. The sucking-face couple took off when I laid a hand on the dude's shoulder as I passed by.

But Dawn didn't notice me. If she had, she would have been long gone. Say what you liked about Dawn Hathaway, but she wasn't dumb, at least not judging by that smart mouth she was always running the handful of times we had encountered each other this semester. She was sitting cross-legged on the floor across from a guy, one I didn't recognize, and they were laughing. She was something to behold as she threw her head back and cackled in delight, her long blond hair flapping out behind her like she was in a shampoo commercial.

I had to tamp that shit down. Yes, Dawn was a lovely girl, but she was also an eighteen-year-old student. An eighteen-year-old student who was about to do a shot.

And since it was nearly twelve-thirty, I was guessing it wasn't her first of the evening.

I walked over to where the pair of them were huddled and stood there without speaking. She threw her head back, not in laughter this time but to swallow the contents of the small glass. Her white throat undulated as she swallowed. There was nothing to mar the endless expanse of porcelain skin, not even a single freckle.

"Mmmm," she said, sticking her tongue out and, good *Lord*, into the shot glass so she could lick every last drop from it.

"Tasty?" I folded my arms across my chest as I moved closer, so I was standing right above her.

The guy she was with scrambled to his feet, but Dawn remained unfazed. "Yes," she said, tilting her head back to look at me as she licked her lips. "You can't beat Baileys."

Well, that was enough of that. "All right, Miss Hathaway. Up and out now, and I won't give you a ticket to add to your collection." In truth, I'd only given her the one, that first week of school, but I had come across her several times the past semester in less-than-savory scenarios. Just last week, I'd apprehended her and some of her friends in the midst of stealing Ace the Allenhurst Anaconda. There was a bronze statue of the school's reptilian mascot mounted above the football field, and students were forever stealing it—in fact, "Ace replacement" was a line item in the college's budget every year.

"Do you celebrate Christmas, Officer Perez?" she asked.

"*Dawn.*" The guy she'd been with grabbed her hand. "Let's *go*."

She pulled herself from his grasp. "It's okay, Tony.

Officer Perez is harmless." Her gaze flickered to my belt. "He doesn't even carry a gun."

I clenched my jaw to keep myself from reacting. An oversize reaction was exactly what she wanted. I didn't know Dawn Hathaway well, but I knew her type. She couldn't stand to be ignored. "Aren't you going to introduce me to your boyfriend?"

"Oh, Tony's not my boyfriend." Dawn made a face like the idea disgusted her. "He's a total player." When he started to protest, she patted him on the shoulder. "Anyway, he only sleeps with older girls."

"Charming." I eyed this Tony kid and made a mental note to keep an eye out for him. He was dressed head to toe in black. Yeah, I knew the type. Listened to "deep" music and made all the girls think he was sensitive and misunderstood. But he was steady on his feet, so I assumed he wasn't too drunk. "But Tony is still going to make sure you get home okay, *right*?" I was talking to her, technically, but I looked at Tony as I spoke.

"Yeah, uh…" Tony's eyes darted around like he was looking for something.

"Ha!" Dawn grinned. "Tony is in deep doo-doo because he just realized he lost his sister, and God forbid his beloved twin should fall prey to a jerk like him." Tony's face said "guilty as charged," and Dawn said, "It's okay, Tony. Go find her. I'll be fine." She scrambled to her feet. "I always am."

Jesus Christ, she was wearing a toga. Only about half the party attendees were. Hers was made from a white sheet fashioned into a minidress that was belted at the waist by a bunch of fake leaves. It crossed over her chest so that one arm and shoulder were completely bare. I cleared my throat, reminding myself that togas were not inherently sexy. They cover more than they reveal, after all. But the idea that she was wearing only a bedsheet that you could probably pull at one end and the whole damn thing would slide off her...

"Merry Christmas, Officer Artie."

Ignoring the liberty she'd taken with my name, I pointed at her—got all in her face with my finger, actually. "You. Wait here. I'm taking you home." Because no way was she going out into the snowy dark night to walk home alone. The Alpha Phi sorority house wasn't far, but still.

"I'm fine," she protested. "That was my only drink of the night."

I let my finger actually make contact with the skin of her chest. Her eyebrows flew up. Good. Because sometimes it seemed like nothing could unsettle this world-weary eighteen-year-old. "Wait. Here." When she opened her mouth like she was going to protest again, I added, "Unless you'd like a second ticket to round out your first semester?"

She shook her head and slumped against the wall in defeat.

Twenty minutes later, after I'd broken up the party sufficiently and collected Dawn, we made our way out into the blessedly cold air. The ivy-covered limestone buildings of frat row were blanketed in freshly fallen snow. It was a gorgeous night, one of those perfect small-town Massachusetts winter nights that I loved. Unlike in Boston, the snow here was clean, and the dry cold had an almost antiseptic effect. I would miss winter in Allenhurst when I finally capitulated and headed home. I glanced at my watch—one-fifteen. Although Dawn didn't know it, as of fifteen minutes ago, I was officially off duty, and for an entire week at that. I was tempted to suggest we walk and I'd come back for the cruiser, but her legs were bare. Man, these kids. How had she gotten here to begin with? So I led her to the car.

"Do I have to sit in the back?"

I answered by opening the front passenger door for her, and she shot me what might have been the first genuine Dawn Hathaway smile I had ever been in receipt of.

"Alpha Phi?" I asked after I'd scraped the ice off the windshield and situated myself in the driver's seat.

"Wilmer Hall," she said, naming a dorm on the other side of campus. "Freshmen don't live in fraternity and sorority houses. The college requires freshmen to live in the dorms. Anyway, it wouldn't work logistically, since pledge period is six weeks. You have to live somewhere while you pledge."

"Right." I had known that, but the ins and outs of Greek life weren't generally front of mind.

"And also?"

I turned to her. The smile from before was gone. She regarded me with annoyed-looking raised eyebrows.

"I didn't get in. I didn't get a bid after rush week. And since I'd focused one hundred per cent on Alpha Phi, I didn't get a bid from any of the other houses, either."

I barked a laugh. I couldn't help it. The idea of Little Miss Dawn not getting something she wanted was oddly satisfying. "I'm sorry," I said through my laughter. "Was it the ticket in September?"

"I'm sure it didn't help." She slumped against her seat,

shoulders curving forward in resignation. "They said I wanted it too much."

"What?"

"And also that I wasn't pretty enough."

"Wait. *What*?"

"Have you seen this year's pledge class? They weren't wrong."

"Are they actually allowed to not let you in based on some subjective measure of beauty?" I was appalled. "To begin with, that's not legal." Also, Dawn Hathaway might have been a pain in my ass, but, with her trim little waist, her small but perfectly proportioned curves, that gorgeous mane of yellow hair, and those killer hazel eyes that were always perfectly made up, she was a *gorgeous* pain in my ass. But of course I wasn't going to say that.

She huffed a bitter laugh. "Yeah, well, no one will admit it to outsiders, but welcome to Greek life."

"Well, you're better off."

She rolled her eyes, which made me feel like I was about fifty years old.

"I don't need them anyway."

"That's the spirit." I stopped at a red light and glanced at her. "Need them for what?" Did she have some kind of secret agenda? She seemed like the type who might.

She started to answer; then she shook her head like she was thinking better of it. "I joined the newspaper. The *Allenhurst Examiner*. You know it?"

Ah, that explained why she'd referred to me as "Officer Artie" earlier. The editor of the paper, Jenny Fields, was always calling me that. I let her get away with it because she was a great kid. She was always fighting for some cause, standing up for the little guy. I often had to break up a protest she was organizing, but we had a lot of respect for each other and had actually developed quite a friendly relationship. "I read it every day," I said, answering Dawn's question truthfully. I wasn't kidding when I told my family that I was part of the community at Allenhurst College. I loved the *Examiner*—it was small but mighty. Although I was frankly shocked that a girl like Dawn would lower herself to do something as serious as journalism.

"I talked them into letting me start a gossip column. It's gonna start spring semester."

Ah. That was more like it.

"So it's actually better that I'm not in a sorority," she said. "If I were, I'd be kind of limited in my gossip range."

"Your gossip range?"

"Yeah. You know, some of those houses are pretty insular. This way I'm kind of a floater."

"A floater?" Listen to me. I had been reduced to repeating everything this girl said as I navigated slowly through the icy streets. But that was because none of it was making any sense.

"Yeah, like, I'm making connections with people who live in all the houses, and some non-Greek people, too." She turned to me, clapping her hands together. She looked like a little girl on Christmas morning. "Gossip is all about connections. Sources. You have those, and you're all set."

"Set for what?"

"Social power."

Jesus. Inside this little blond girl there was a Machiavellian schemer.

"So I really *wasn't* drinking at that party," she went on. "Tony—he's a photographer at the newspaper—talked me into doing that one shot you saw, but it would have stopped there." She cocked her head and smirked. "It turns out if you're the only sober one in a party full of wastoids, you can get a lot of info."

Wow. It wasn't that I thought she was stupid. I'd never thought that. But maybe she had more real wisdom than I'd given her credit for. "You headed home for the holidays?" I asked, suddenly interested in what kind of background had spawned this beautiful young mercenary.

"Unfortunately." I raised my eyebrows, and she sighed. "I don't have the best relationship with my father and stepmother."

"Where's home?"

"New York City."

"What about your mother?"

"There is no mother. And Daddy is…busy."

I wanted to ask more, and I almost did. I told myself that my questions were rooted in my commitment to community policing. That this was a prime example of why I hung on at Allenhurst despite the almost-unendurable pressure from my family to join "the family business," aka the Boston PD, where my father, brother, and one sister served. I didn't want to be just a warm body with a gun chasing after bad guys who had already done the deed. Not that there was anything wrong with that, but for me policing was about people. About hearing their stories and helping them make good choices. And I felt like the kids here were at an age where it was still possible to make a difference in their lives.

Still, I was pretty sure my interest in Dawn's background wasn't about being a good community cop. *What does "busy" mean? Do you have any step-siblings? What do you mean "there is no mother"? That's not biologically possible.*

"It's like he doesn't even see me, you know?"

This happened sometimes with these kids. They

needed someone to talk to, and sometimes it only took the slightest nudge to open the tap. We had arrived at her dorm. I pulled up in front and cut the engine.

"It doesn't matter what I do," she went on, making no move to get out or even seeming to register that we had arrived. "Good grades, bad grades." She made it sound like she'd tried both. "Tickets for underage drinking." She rolled her eyes, and I couldn't help but chuckle. "He just never…*sees* me."

It seemed impossible that anyone could be in proximity to Dawn Hathaway and not see her—hell, not be pretty much all-consumed by her. She took up so much space, in spite of her petite build. But I couldn't say that. And maybe what she was saying was true. There were a lot of shitty parents out there.

"Ugh!" She waved a hand in front of her face as if she were disgusted with herself. "Listen to me. I'm exhausted from exams, and I'm getting maudlin." She unbuckled her seat belt and pulled on her mittens. I had to laugh at the combination of her heavy, knitted mittens and her mini-toga. "Anyway, not being seen turns out to be a real advantage in the gossip business, so it all works out. Thanks for the ride." She hopped out of the car but leaned back down to look in. "And thanks for not giving me another ticket." She smiled—my second real Dawn Hathaway smile—then slammed the door. I watched her sashay her toga-covered ass up the path to the dorm's front door.

And with that, I put another semester—my thirteenth; wouldn't Dad be thrilled?—at Allenhurst to bed.

CHAPTER THREE

May 1982

DAWN

"Goddamn it! Hurry *up*, Dawn!"

I looked down from my perch above the football stadium to see Tony raking his hands through his hair and staring down the block as he bounced on his toes like an agitated prizefighter. I couldn't see what he was looking at. From my vantage point, the view was blocked by the pedestal that was Ace's home, which rested high above the stadium gates. Or the pedestal that *had* been Ace's home—my trusty crowbar and I were nearly done prying him loose.

"Gotcha!" I said, relishing my victory. An Ace was serious currency around campus.

"I think that's my line," said an all-too-familiar voice.

I braced myself for the body that belonged to the voice to step into view.

And there he was, a wall of muscle with his mirrored

shades on, even though it was overcast.

Damn. Was this guy *everywhere*? Why was he always catching me red-handed? It didn't matter where the party was, what the prank was, *he always knew*. And why was it always *him*? The police force at Allenhurst employed eight officers. I knew, because I'd checked. Before Jenny, the editor of the school paper, would let me have my gossip column, she'd made me write a story for each of the paper's sections. It was this dumb rule she had—if you weren't a journalism major, you had to "do time" in each section before you settled into your beat. It was supposed to give us sympathy for how the other sections operated or something. Anyway, while on general news, I'd done a story about the police department's new cruisers. They'd replaced their two AMC Matadors with Chevy Caprices. Ooh la la, stop the presses.

Somehow, Jenny's little rule never resulted in anyone rotating through the gossip page, which was fine by me. Since I'd launched the column, the paper's circulation had quadrupled. And it wasn't because of stories about the new cop cars. Yeah, Jenny might have been the editor of the paper, but I was its star.

Anyway, the point was there were eight cops at this school, and six thousand students. So why the heck was Officer Perez—I tried to call him Officer Artie once, like Jenny did, but it felt *wrong*—the one always busting my ass?

My ass that was in real trouble at the moment. There was no way to spin this one. I was on top of one of the huge pillars that bracketed the stadium, and I had a crowbar in one hand and our school's mascot in the other. At least from this vantage point, Officer Perez wasn't his usual gigantic self, taking up all my space and air.

But, actually, he still kind of was, as impossible as it should have been. I had to drop the crowbar because I was feeling a little dizzy. I clawed at the brick, panicking a moment before I grabbed solidly hold of it.

"For fuck's sake, Dawn, be careful!" Wow. I'd never heard Officer Perez swear or even lose his cool. I'd also never heard him call me Dawn. It was nearly the end of sophomore year. So for two school years, it had always been Miss Hathaway. "It's about to start pouring," he said, and boy was he irritated.

Before I could say anything—or even blink—he had scaled the gate and was next to me doing his air-sucking and space-taking thing from closer proximity.

"How the hell did you get up here?" he demanded, his eyes blazing. He had taken off his shades, so I could see his eyes, which almost never happened. I leaned in to get a better look. The only other time I'd seen him without his glasses was when he'd driven me home after the Delta Chi Christmas party my freshman year. I'd kicked myself later for not noticing what color his eyes were.

They were brown. Not that that was a surprise, given his apparently Latino heritage. But I'd wanted to know what kind of brown. The answer was a warm medium brown flecked with that tiniest bits of moss green, like oxidized pennies.

"How did you get up here?" he repeated, his voice going all low and growly this time.

"Um, the same way you did?" I ventured. I wanted to say that I was actually an expert at scaling these gates. That even though he had only caught me twice, this was my fourth Ace theft. I should have waited for the middle of the night this time. I was getting overconfident. I had been impatient because this Ace was going to win me the scoop of the semester. Or *would* have, had the long arm of the law not arrived.

The long *arms*, plural, which were currently snaking around me. And they were such nice arms, really, if you could set aside the fact that they were probably going to arrest me once we hit the pavement.

"Drop the snake, Miss Hathaway," he ordered. "We're heading down."

I tried—and failed—to shrug out of his grasp. "You're not a fireman, Officer Perez. I can climb down by myself." As was so often the case, Officer Unfriendly appeared unmoved by my logic. "You can hardly throw me over your shoulder like a sack of potatoes and—ooof."

Apparently he could. Stubbornly, I kept hold of Ace, though I did let the crowbar clatter to the ground—the ground I noticed was conveniently devoid of Tony, my partner in crime and the one with the umbrellas in his bag in case the sky opened up as it had been threatening all day. The *weasel*.

A clap of thunder punctuated our descent.

When Officer Perez's feet hit the ground, he didn't release me right away. As the rain started, he loosened his grip just enough that I started sliding down his body—his body, I couldn't help noticing, that was as hard as granite. Many of the boys in my class who weren't athletes were sprouting little paunches. The Freshman Fifteen had been real, and some of them had gained another Sophomore Six. But there was none of that going on here. This guy was one solid mass of muscle.

I shivered as he lowered me the last couple of inches to the ground.

"Jesus Christ," he snapped, taking off his windbreaker and throwing it over my shoulders as lightning lanced across the sky and the raindrops grew fatter. "If you're going to commit larceny, at least dress for it."

Larceny. Crap. That sounded bad. Underage drinking was one thing. It was almost expected in college, unless you were a total loser. I wasn't entirely sure how I would spin larceny with Daddy. But the silver lining, I supposed, was that he might have to actually pay attention to me for longer than it took to write a check.

"Why the hell do you kids all care so much about these pieces of junk?" Officer Perez asked, tugging Ace from my grip. And he did have to tug. Damn, I needed that snake. My column was going super well. When I got to my morning classes, everyone was always reading it and exclaiming over its contents. If I could get the story I was currently chasing, even Daddy would have to be impressed. Maybe *especially* Daddy, given how much he liked to talk about how he'd worked his way up from the journalistic trenches to get where he was today.

But of course I was no match for the human mountain. And it wasn't like he was going to let me keep the spoils of the larceny he was about to charge me with. So I opted for the truth. "Don't take this the wrong way—I don't mean to malign your gender or anything—but college boys are stupid."

"Ah, one thing we agree on." He had taken his glasses off to scale the stadium, and now he was putting them back on, which was more disappointing than it should have been. But leave it to Officer Perez to wear sunglasses in a storm. He seemed totally impervious to the rain, which was coming down in earnest now.

I pressed onward. "There's a certain species of boy for whom Ace the Anaconda is, like, a badge of honor. They collect Aces." I shrugged when he scoffed. "I said it was stupid. Anyway, Aces are like currency. I do the gossip column in the paper, you remember?"

"Yes. 'Dish from Dawn,'" he said. Wow. I was, frankly, shocked that he knew it. His skeptical-bordering-on-disgusted tone suggested that he was not a fan, but still.

"Well, I'm *this* close"—I held up my thumb and forefinger—"to a huge scoop. But my source requires payment."

He took his glasses off again—score!—and leaned in, squinting like I was a puzzle he was trying to solve. There were raindrops on his long, dark eyelashes, and I was seized with the absurd desire to reach out and flick them away.

"Let me get this straight," he said. "You are stealing a metal snake *in a lightning storm* in order to use it as payment to secure a piece of gossip that you are going to print in the college newspaper."

God. It sounded so tawdry when he put it like that. "I don't print gossip," I said weakly, trotting out the rationale I used with Jenny, who was constantly wondering aloud how she had lowered her journalistic standards such that she'd ever green-lighted my column. "I require verification of the stories I print, and they often speak truth to power."

The glasses were back on, obscuring his pretty eyes, but his snort was enough to convey his disgust. Well, what did I care what this gunless beefcake of a cop thought of me? "All right, so let's get this show on the road," I said. "If you're actually charging me with larceny, I'm sure my father will want me to get a lawyer before anything happens. So I'll call him from the station." I looked around for his cruiser. "I do get a phone call, right? That's not just on *Starsky and Hutch*?"

"This would be the father who never sees you?" he

asked. Rivulets of water ran down his face, and his already dark hair turned straight-up black as it got wet.

Hot embarrassment pricked my cheeks despite the cold rain. I had no idea why I'd told him that last year, except maybe that I had been a lonely freshman, still reeling from not getting a bid from Alpha Phi and afraid that I'd be a nobody on this campus. Obviously, I needn't have worried. Dish with Dawn had made me more popular than membership in any sorority would have. Everything was going exactly as I'd hoped.

"Who's your father?" he asked.

"How does that matter?" When he didn't answer, I countered with my own question. "Who's *your* father?" But the minute it was out of my mouth, I regretted it. I'd been covering my embarrassment with belligerence, but I sounded like a spoiled child. Which probably wasn't too far off the mark, but I didn't like the idea of Officer Perez thinking of me that way.

"My father is Emilio Perez," he answered immediately, "lieutenant detective, Boston PD. First-generation American. You should thank your lucky stars you've got me here and not him. If he was here right now, he'd eat you for breakfast."

Shame flooded me, and it was enough to prompt me to answer his question. "My father is Edward Hathaway. He owns some TV stations." I was understating it. My father was the head of a media empire, a third-generation billionaire, even if he did like to pretend that his decade of reporting for various B-list newspapers—his father had insisted on it before handing over the reins of the company—somehow gave him street cred in the industry.

"Hathaway Media," Officer Perez said. "You own SBC and the *Boston Voice*."

Among other things. I nodded. "Not me, though. My father." I wasn't sure why I was making a point of drawing the distinction. I *wanted* my father to notice me, to remember that I was his, so why was I so intent on making sure Officer Perez knew the difference between me and him?

The way Officer Perez's lip curled as he picked up my crowbar from the sidewalk made me want to shrivel up and die. When he finally spoke, his tone was clipped. "All right, Miss Hathaway. We're done here."

Without waiting for a response, he turned and headed for his car, which was parked half a block down from the stadium—so that was how he'd been able to sneak up on us. Like a dumb wet puppy, I followed him.

He popped the trunk and dropped Ace and the crowbar into it. Then he took off those glasses again—why was he being so uncharacteristically free with his glasses?—and looked me up and down. It was a slow assessment that made me want to squirm, especially because it was now wet enough that my denim cutoffs and halter top were plastered to my body. If that look had been coming from one of the frat guys, I would have called him out on it. But I kept my mouth shut.

"Was there some part of 'we're done here,' that you didn't understand?" he finally said, as if he was lowering himself to explain a very simple concept to a very simple person.

"Oh, okay. Um, thanks?" I said, apparently having morphed into a very simple person to meet his expectations.

Then he got in his car, turned on the flashers, and drove away, leaving me shivering in his Allenhurst College PD windbreaker.

CHAPTER FOUR

September 1982

DAWN

The first day of orientation week I was out and about, strolling the campus with my ear to the ground. The first Dish with Dawn column of the year wouldn't run for another week, but I wanted to find out what everyone was up to and get a sense of the incoming class. My gossip mill had run pretty dry over the summer. I had heard the freshman class included a famous teen actress, and if it was true, I wanted to be the first to report on her.

As I made my way into the roundabout that show-cased the campus's oldest, most stately buildings and its iconic clock tower, my attention was drawn by a crowd. It wasn't the usual crowd though. I squinted. Right. It was parents. The school ran orientation activities for parents who were dropping their freshmen off. Daddy had, of course, not attended. He hadn't even dropped me off—

just left me a wad of cash and a plane ticket in the New York apartment.

A student orientation leader wearing an Allenhurst T-shirt was speaking to a group of parents. Actually, it looked more like she was trying to move them along. Something was holding their attention. No, some*one*— there was a person in the middle of the parental throng.

"Ha!" I laughed to myself as I trotted up to the edge of the group.

It was Officer Unfriendly, and he was surrounded by parents. Well, actually, he was surrounded by mothers. The few fathers in the group were standing in a cluster to one side. Officer Perez was taller than all of them, and his usual steady, substantial presence surrounded by their chattering put me in mind of a mother bird surrounded by squawking babies.

"I, for one, feel so much better knowing someone like you is looking after our children, officer," one of the women purred as she touched his arm.

Ugh. Grody.

He smiled, but anyone could tell it was a fake smile. He was tolerating her but only just.

"Tell us again about your philosophy of community policing," said another, a woman with bright red lips and a wall of hair that told me she was trying awfully, awfully hard to appear young and cool. "I find it so fascinating."

Officer Perez pressed his lips together like he was trying to prevent himself from saying something he would regret.

"*Sí, señor,*" trilled a third. "Me too!"

And: nope. Officer Perez might be my nemesis, but I wasn't going to stand here and let these middle-aged harpies fetishize him.

"Officer Perez!" I called, shouldering my way through the well-manicured rabble.

He looked up, and I swear, for one second he looked happy to see me. Then his face hardened into something closer to wariness. Whatever. I might not be his ideal knight in shining armor, but I was going in whether he liked it or not. I pressed on.

"There's a little problem in the..." I looked over my shoulder to orient myself. "In the art building. We need your help." I flashed my best smile at him. "So sorry, everyone," I said, taking his forearm and pulling him toward me. I'm not really sure how I had the guts to actually touch him. But he came with me.

"Enjoy your empty nests, ladies," I tossed over my shoulder, sneaking a glance at him as I spoke.

He was pressing his lips together again, but this time it seemed like it was because he was trying not to laugh.

We didn't speak until we'd rounded the corner of the art building and were out of sight.

"Thanks," he said, letting the grin he'd been suppressing out of hiding.

I shrugged, but I was absurdly pleased to have done something he appreciated for once. "I guess even cops need rescuing sometimes."

"Giving the campus safety talk at parent orientation is the worst. I drew the short straw this year."

"Well, what a bunch of airheads. Gag me."

"Can I walk you somewhere?" he asked, looking at his watch.

"Nope. I'm drifting around a bit, getting the lay of the land now that school's back in session."

"Trolling for gossip, you mean." He smirked. I would

have thought he was teasing me, but I was pretty sure Officer Perez didn't tease.

It was true, but it made me sound so shallow, and after seeing those women in action just now, I didn't want him to think of me that way. But what could I do but brush the comment off? "Potato, potahto."

"You did some good things with that column toward the end of last year," he said, and I couldn't have been more shocked if he'd slapped handcuffs on me and arrested me on the spot.

He started to walk away, and I wanted to run after him and ask him to elaborate. The need to hear from Officer Perez's mouth the good things I'd done was almost visceral. But that was dumb. So, instead, I said, "Have you heard anything about Jolie Fosting starting here as a student?"

He cocked his head and flashed me a full-on smile, which was more jolting than it should have been. "I have no idea what you're talking about."

He was lying, but what could I do but smile back at him? He turned to leave, and I watched his broad shoulders as he retreated. As impossible as it seemed, I'd kind of missed seeing him this summer.

How embarrassing, then, when he turned back and caught me staring.

"I'll see you at Delta Chi on Friday?" he asked.

Right. The annual back-to-school bash. I suppressed another smile—man, I was smiling a lot today. It was weird. "I have no idea what you're talking about."

ARTURO

I came with a partner this year because the word on the street was that Delta Chi's back-to-school party was going to be bigger than ever. Kegs were one thing, but cocaine was another, and we'd been finding it more and more on campus, so we were taking an aggressive approach—doing more in pairs, making our presence known earlier and more aggressively than we might have a year ago. We only waited for the first noise complaint before my partner, Fuller, and I headed out.

As we made our way up the path to the front door, it wasn't lost on me that I wasn't supposed to be here. Two years ago, I'd assured Dad—and everyone else—that I was going to finish out that academic year, then resign and come home. Dad had been thrilled that I was finally done with my "little detour," and talked excitedly about lining me up with interviews for the Boston force.

But here I was. One year had become two. Because I just...hadn't made the break. Kept putting it off. I tried telling everyone at home the truth: I liked it here. I was doing good work. But it was never enough. So I always added that after one more year, I'd hang it up. And, hey, I thought bitterly, maybe next time Dad decided to ride my ass about it, I could tell him about the rash of cocaine busts on campus. Maybe if he thought things were getting semi-hard-core, he'd decide that Allenhurst was "worthy of my talents and my family legacy," and get the hell off my back.

It was only midnight, so things were not as out of hand at the party as they could have been. Fuller, who was younger and was one of those guys who seemed like he'd gone into policing because he was on some kind of power trip, usually went into a bust like this with his dick swinging. Which was fine—it made my life easier, frankly. So I hung back a little and let him play Bad Cop. Contrary to rumor, there was no coke at the party, at least not on the main level, so he went around checking IDs and writing up kids for possession while I looked around for Dawn.

Yeah, I wasn't even going to try to deny it to myself. I needed to lay eyes on her. Every single party I busted, every post-football-game bonfire, every parent-orientation tour, she was always there working her connections in service of her column, and I'd gotten into this mindset where I needed to make sure she was okay. She always was, of course. But I had to check. I always had to check. Because something told me that she wasn't actually okay, not really. So I would seek her out, make eye contact, and then go on my way. I wasn't sure why I was so compelled to look out for her, except it seemed like maybe no one else was. She was at the center of everything, but she was also alone.

Tonight, she was nowhere to be seen. A niggle of worry gnawed at me as my initial sweep of the main floor failed to yield a glimpse of her. Earlier, she'd all but admitted she was coming. There was no way Dawn would miss a Delta Chi party. And when she was at these things, she was always on the main level, the calm eye of the storm, the sober, well-dressed one who made her colleagues look like overgrown, sloppy children. I always made sure to read her column after one of these parties. I usually read it anyway, but it was always funny to see something and then read about it later though her eyes. Her column was funny—and smart, though I never thought I'd say that about a gossip column. I thought she had been blowing smoke when she claimed she spoke truth to power, but she kind of did. She sent up the Greek system, for example, even as she reported on it.

And she'd printed a series of blind items about an asshole football player preying on freshman girls that had caused the school to investigate and ended up getting him kicked off the team. That had impressed the hell out of me.

And the column seemed to have gotten her what she wanted: social power. That was the phrase she had used when I drove her home from one of these parties a couple years ago. Every time I saw her in action, she was the belle of the ball. Everyone wanted her attention, and she moved through these sorts of parties with a kind of bemused grace, like the queen that she was. She always wore black —when she wasn't wearing a toga—and she looked like she was a decade more mature than all her neon-hued peers.

I scanned the crowd again and came up empty, except I did spot that Tony kid—the Gothy jerk who had bailed on her when I busted her for her Ace the Anaconda caper last spring. What kind of asshole hung his friend—girl-friend? God I hoped not—out to dry like that? He tried to turn tail when I approached, but I grabbed the lapel of his coat. "Where's Dawn?"

"She's around."

"Can you be a little more specific?"

"She went upstairs a few minutes ago," said Jenny Fields, whom I hadn't noticed on the other side of Tony, probably because she was the last type of kid I'd expect to find at a raging frat party.

She must have interpreted my raised eyebrows correctly, because she shrugged and said, "Sometimes you gotta see how the other half lives." But then she leaned in close and said, "Dawn went upstairs with that creep Royce Waldorf. Do you know him?"

I didn't pause long enough to answer her; I just hit the stairs.

DAWN

Royce Waldorf was a creep. Everyone knew it. He'd been hitting on me since that first party I went to freshman year. Heck, he'd been hitting on everything that moved. And it was his fifth year, so why was he even still here? Of course, the answer to that was probably because he'd partied so much he didn't have enough credits to graduate on time.

Anyway, as much as Royce gave me the heebie-jeebies there was no way I was going to turn down his invitation to chat privately about some "serious gossip" he claimed to be sitting on. Honestly, if anyone was going to have some good dirt, it was Royce Waldorf. Not only was he a scumbag who ran with scumbags, he was a rich, well-connected scumbag. An Izod-and-Swatch-wearing scumbag, but a scumbag nonetheless. And he'd spent the fall interning for one of his dad's colleagues in the Senate. I'm not going to lie; I was having visions of Dish with Dawn breaking open the next Watergate. Daddy would pee his pants.

I thought I could handle Royce, but I was beginning to wonder if I'd been wrong. I had made the mistake of letting him hold the door for me—we were in his upstairs bedroom so he could tell me his super-secret dirt in private—but that meant he was between me and the door.

And he was very, very drunk. Maybe even high. I didn't have a lot of experience with drugs, but it seemed like he had more than booze in his system.

"I've been trying to get you up here for two years," he slurred.

"So what's your news, Royce?" I said, trying to keep him on track.

"It will cost you."

"I don't pay my sources." Not anymore, anyway.

"Renee Williamson had a nose job."

"I know that."

He reared back with a degree of shock that was way out of proportion to the situation and probably attributable to his degree of inebriation. It would have been funny in another setting.

"So why haven't you printed it?"

"I don't do that kind of gossip." It was true. I hadn't ever articulated it in my speeches to Jenny about the redeeming value of gossip, but I didn't print things that had no purpose other than to be outright mean. Or at least I didn't anymore. I'd done a couple items in the early days of my column that had left me with a bad taste in my mouth. One was about a girl who showed up to my Intro to Social Psych lecture every day in the same clothes. Every single day. I didn't say her name or print a picture, but it was easy enough to figure out who she was. I thought I was making amusing remarks about her (lack of) fashion sense, but I found out later that she was on a scholarship and lived in a boardinghouse. There had been no point in running that item. So now, I only ran items about people who should know better doing shit they shouldn't be doing. Hypocrites. People abusing power. Arrogant dickheads who needed to be taken down a peg. The distinction was probably lost on my readers, though. Everyone thought of me as the shallow campus gossip. But, hey, at least they thought of me. "So if that's all..." I tried to brush past Royce, but he stuck out an arm and blocked me.

"I saw Professor Daniels from the communication department making out with an undergrad."

Adrenaline flooded my system. I wanted that. Oh, how I wanted that story. I'd been onto it a year ago. That was when I'd first started hearing rumblings about this prof coming onto students, but I'd never been able to come up with anything definitive. In fact, that had been what I'd been stealing the damned mascot for that day Officer Perez caught me. One of Royce's buddies had been dangling hints—a lot of the Delta Chi boys were comm majors because the courses were so easy—and he'd told me to bring him Ace. That was actually when I had instituted the "I don't pay my sources" rule. Once I thought about it, I realized I'd been scrambling around like a common criminal trying to steal a metal snake to give to a frat boy. No wonder Officer Perez had been so disgusted. It was unseemly. And ironically, like playing hard to get, not paying my sources—and not running every item that was brought to me—had only made me more popular. If anything, people sought me out more than they used to with secrets and tips.

But this Daniels story would be huge. It would go way beyond gossip. If I had a source willing to go on the record, it would be front-page news. When I'd done a story about a football player who basically date-raped his way through the freshman class, Jenny had run Dish with Dawn on the front page. We had struck a bargain: I would get to keep the column's branding and first-person voice, and she would help me edit the piece into more of a mainstream news story that would be serious and hard-hitting enough to justify the claims I was making. She had put me through the wringer, requiring documentation of sources and even consulting with a lawyer. But the story had been airtight. The school hadn't responded very quickly or very rigorously, and that had sparked protests. Eventually, the football player had been expelled. I'm not going to lie; it was a bit of a thrill to see Dish with Dawn on the front page—and then in the rest of the regional media outlets that reported on the story.

A professor abusing his power and preying on students would be even bigger than the football-player story. I didn't have mainstream journalistic ambitions, but, heck, maybe I should get some, because the idea of taking down Daniels in a similar fashion was now all I could think about. It also hadn't escaped my attention that breaking a story like that would *really* get my media mogul father's attention. The football player had merited a brief mention. But this? He'd probably try to hand me the editorship of one of his papers, which was not something I was interested in, but at least it would mean he knew I was alive.

Royce laughed. Crap. He could sense how desperately I wanted the story. On unsteady feet, he lurched toward me. "I'm not going to make you sleep with me, but you gotta give me something."

"Excuse me? I have to *give you something*?" Eff that. I was done with this conversation. I'd find another way to get to Daniels. If someone as dumb as Royce Waldorf knew about it, so did other people. And I would find them.

"Yeah, you know, a little tit for tat." He guffawed. "Ha! Tit!"

God. Did the imbecile not see the irony in trying to blackmail me into sleeping with him as payment for information about a professor…blackmailing a student to sleep with him?

"Show me your tits at least, and we'll go from there."

We'll go from there? Scoffing, but starting to get a tiny bit nervous, I made another effort to get past him. His arm shot out again, and he grabbed my wrist. Coming up here with him had been a mistake. "Let go of me, you dickweed!" I spat, twisting out of his grasp. I lunged for the door, but not fast enough, and now he was mad.

"You fucking whore. You parade around in your little black dresses like you're so mature. You think you're too good for everyone."

I tried to brazen my way through the shock of his cutting words. "I'm too good for *you*, that's for sure."

"You've been leading me on for two years. I'm not going to—"

This was not going to happen. I thought I had been flooded with adrenaline before, but I'd had no idea. I retracted my leg and kneed him in the groin for all I was worth at the same time shouting, "Help! I need help!"

"Dawn?" called an answering voice from the hallway, a low one I felt like I should know but couldn't quite place.

But it didn't matter. Anyone was better than Royce. Out there was better than in here.

"I'm in the first bedroom on the left, and I need help," I yelled, even as I finally shoved my way past Royce, who was still writhing in pain and cursing me out. As I turned the doorknob, someone pushed the door in from the outside and I fell onto my ass—but only for a second because, almost fast enough to give me whiplash, I felt myself propelled upward and pulled into a strong embrace. At first I thought it was Royce, and I screamed.

"Dawn! It's me!" I struggled against powerful arms

holding me against an unyielding chest. "It's Arturo Perez, Allenhurst College PD."

Officer Unfriendly. Of course. I should have known those arms.

And as fast as my body had been deluged with adrenaline before, all the fight left me. It was like I was an over-inflated balloon that sprang a leak. I started shaking—and crying—as I sagged against his chest. A small part of my rational mind that was still hanging on knew I was completely overreacting, but I couldn't stop. It was like I couldn't get a hold of myself—or of anything. Like I was the escaped helium from that balloon, floating uncontained into the atmosphere, losing more and more of myself with every second.

Officer Perez kept repeating my name, and not the "Miss Hathaway" version of it he had used in the past. "Dawn. Dawn." Then he pulled me off his chest, holding me far enough away that he could look in my eyes. "Dawn," he said again, very low, almost whispering, but with an urgency that made it seem like he was shouting. "I see you, Dawn. I see you."

ARTURO

Hadn't I just been thinking that I wasn't one of those cops in it for power, for vengeance? Well, the joke was on me, because as soon as I knew Dawn was stabilized and unhurt —physically, at least—I jumped all over Royce fucking Waldorf like I was the one with cocaine whishing around in my veins. I called for Fuller and had Waldorf cuffed and on the floor under my knee before my colleague made it up the stairs.

His eyes widened when he took in the scene. "Whatcha got here?"

"Where's the coke?" I asked Royce.

"Do you know who my father is?" he shouted.

"Save that shit for the judge," I said. "Doesn't work on me."

Fuller had started rummaging through the desk, and it wasn't a second before he turned up a white-powder-filled baggie. "Bingo." Fuller grinned. "You want me to take him back and charge him?"

"Yes. We may also have other charges, too." I glanced at Dawn. She shook her head. I wanted to urge her not to fold, but I couldn't blame her. Sexual-assault charges were hard enough for the victim, and we all knew who Royce's father was. But since she could always press charges later, I decided my priority was to get her out of there.

Five minutes later, I was settling her into my car. We hadn't been able to find her coat in the huge pile at the party, and she'd assured me she would be able to get it from one of the Alpha Phi girls. But she was only wearing a sleeveless black minidress, so she was shivering. It was September, but the nights were getting cool. So I shrugged out of my leather jacket and settled it over her shoulders. "Do you need me to, ah, take you to the hospital?" I asked gently when I'd come around and strapped myself into the driver's seat.

She shook her head as she stared out the window. "Nothing happened."

"Didn't seem like nothing."

She huffed a bitter laugh. "My reaction was way out of proportion." She turned to look at me, and I wanted to crumple when I saw how sad her eyes were. "I'm sorry."

"No."

I must have spoken too loudly, too decisively, because she flinched a little, which made me feel like absolute shit.

I shook my head. "I only meant there's no reason for you to be sorry. About anything."

Another bitter laugh. "Well, I wouldn't go that far."

"Royce Waldorf is an entitled, cowardly bully of a simpleton," I said, and that drew a small smile, so I went on. "So even if he didn't physically touch you, it wasn't 'nothing.' You can still press him on attempted assault."

"No way," she said quickly. "I just want to forget this."

I nodded and pulled away from frat row. I almost lost control of the car when she said, "Thank you for rescuing me. I'm so lucky you were there. It was like he had super-human strength or something."

"That was the coke, probably. But you were on your way out of that room when I got there." It was true. "You rescued yourself."

"Still," said Dawn. "I'm glad you were there. Glad it was *you* who was there."

My cheeks went hot, and my collar was suddenly too tight. Jesus Christ, was I blushing? Thank God it was dark.

"Wilmer Hall, still?" I asked.

"Nope," she said. "I'm in an apartment now. Two-fifty-two Marlin Street."

We passed the short drive in silence. When I pulled up in front of her building, I cut the engine and turned to her. "Is your roommate home?"

"I live alone."

"Oh." It was unusual for undergraduate students to live alone. They were like pack animals at this age. And Dawn was such a social creature. "Are you sure I can't take you somewhere else? To a friend's place, maybe?"

She shook her head. "I'll be okay."

I wasn't convinced, but I couldn't force the issue. For once, she hadn't done anything wrong. So I pulled out a business card and a pen. "This is my card. I'm adding my home number to it. You call me anytime you need anything, okay? *Anytime*."

She nodded and took the card. She was being so agreeable. It was…unsettling.

But not as unsettling as what happened next. She unbuckled her seat belt, leaned across the car, and placed her lips on mine.

I should have pushed her away immediately. But I considered the fact that I remained still a small victory. Hell, sitting there impassively while she brushed an almost-chaste kiss across my lips while my body burst into flames wasn't a *small* victory. It was a huge one. I wanted to grab the sides of her face. I wanted to push her mouth open with my tongue. I wanted…things that I couldn't want. Things that were impossible.

Her lips were soft and tentative as they opened slightly, and her tongue came out and tested the seam of my lips.

I groaned, but I did manage to push her away then, and I did so as gently as I could. She was in shock. She didn't know what she was doing. She was acting out. I told myself all those things. I told my *dick* all those things, because it, too, was acting out.

I would have expected her to be embarrassed, to apologize, or blush, or…something. But she gazed at me evenly, sad hazel eyes searching my face like it held answers. Then she finally said, once again, "Thank you," got out of the car, and walked up the path to the front door of her building, dwarfed by my too-big jacket.

CHAPTER FIVE

May 1983

ARTURO

I saw her the moment we set foot in the bar. I'd recognize that teased blond hair anywhere, the signature black dress —this one was sleeveless and decorated with zigzagging zippers across the bodice. Dawn was small, but at the same time, she was impossible to miss. She was huddled at the bar with a girlfriend, a barely touched pint of beer in front of her. I wondered if she was "working." I thought about her living alone and wondered if she had any genuine friends or if she was too busy maintaining her "social power" for that.

Dawn didn't see me, but I drew more than my share of glances as I made my way through the dim bar.

This was why I made a point of never going to campus bars. If I wanted to drink, I went to a watering hole the next town over, I held out until my weekly poker night with a bunch of guys I knew in town, or I made the ninety-minute drive to Boston to hang with my high school buddies and crashed at my parents' house. It wasn't like I was a celebrity on campus or anything, but enough people knew me that I preferred to keep my personal shit out of sight in Allenhurst.

But I'd come home earlier that night to a blinking answering machine full of messages from my brother Manuel. He was driving up to meet me, said the first one, which was weird. Manny and I were close enough—hell, I'd take a bullet for any of my siblings—but we didn't go out of our way to see each other. The second was from a pay phone outside my apartment, the third from outside the campus police services building. We'd kept missing each other. Well, he'd kept missing me—until I got home, I didn't know he was looking for me. The last of the four messages proclaimed that he was settling in at the Allenhurst Tap Room and instructed me to come meet him as soon as I could. And leave it to Manny to gravitate to the grungiest, cheapest watering hole on campus. There was a reason everyone called this bar "the A-Hole." I had been here enough times breaking up fights that I generally saw no call to darken its door as a patron.

But family first. That was the unofficial Perez family motto, drilled into us by our father. And to be fair, it had served my brother and me and our two sisters well growing up. As one of the only Puerto Rican families in our working-class Irish neighborhood, we were sometimes out of our element, so we'd tended to stick together. *Family first.* And there was no shaking it now.

Realizing I'd been so caught up in looking at Dawn that I hadn't found my brother, I scanned the bar more purposefully.

Manny was sitting a few spots down the bar from Dawn. Of course.

They both turned as I approached.

Dawn threw her hands in the air like she was a bank teller and I was a thief. "I'm legal now!" she shouted, louder than was necessary, because it was early and the bar wasn't buzzing yet.

I had to suppress a grin. "And I'm off duty now."

Her mouth fell open as she took in my street clothes. Ha. In the same way that little kids think their teachers sleep at school, she had probably never thought of me as a civilian. I edged in on Manny's other side, leaving two empty stools between her and my brother. I hadn't had any run-ins with Dawn lately. Well, not any run-ins where we talked. But I'd seen plenty of her. More than she knew, in fact. If I'd looked for her before, at parties and games and campus events, I was even more vigilant since the night Royce Waldorf attacked her, scanning every crowd for the black-clothing/blond-hair combination that was her trademark.

My vigilance wasn't about Royce himself, though he was back on campus. He'd slithered out of the drug charges—no surprise there—and was finishing his fifth year. He had done enough partying that he hadn't graduated in the usual four. I could only pray that this year would be his last. Still, I had a hunch that Royce was done with Dawn. She'd shown him up—she'd won—and I somehow knew he wouldn't be bothering her anymore. So I wasn't protecting Dawn from Royce, exactly. I was protecting her from…everything. Or trying to, anyway. Which I realized made no sense, but it was what it was.

I'd even taken to driving the cruiser past her building at night. Once, I was driving by as she was coming home, so I was able to wait and watch and, when I saw a third-floor light flip on, identify which apartment was hers. Now, if it was off when I drove by on patrol in the evenings, I got antsy.

"Hey," I said to Manny, shaking myself out of my thoughts as I accepted a beer from the bartender.

"Pops had a heart attack," he said.

I spilled my beer. "Jesus Christ, *what*?"

"It was just a little one. He's having an angioplasty tomorrow. It's like they blow up a balloon in his vein or some shit."

"Fuck, Manny, why didn't anyone *tell* me? When did this happen?"

He held up his hands like Dawn had a minute ago. I was aware that I was yelling, which was ironic because I'd purposely sat on this side of him—the non-Dawn side—to give us some privacy. I didn't need the denizens of Allenhurst knowing my business. I had a reputation of omniscience to maintain.

"Yesterday. And I'm telling you now. We didn't think you should hear it over the phone."

I heard what he wasn't saying. *You weren't there.*

"Anyway, he's going to be okay." Manny grinned. "Well, he's going to have to stop smoking and start eating vegetables and shit, which he is *not* happy about, but they say with lifestyle changes and some medicine, he should make a decent recovery."

I started pulling paper napkins from a dispenser on the bar and using them to try to mop up my spilled beer. Manny stopped me by putting his hand on my arm.

"I was scared out of my mind for a moment there, Art. We were sitting there watching the Red Sox beat the shit

46

out of the Tigers, and he stood up and started clutching his chest like in the movies."

My throat was thick, and I had to swallow to get any words out. "I'm sorry," I said, though I wasn't sure what I was apologizing for—for not being there like I should have been, I guess.

"The last thing he said before the ambulance took him away was to tell you to come home."

"I'll get some time off and come tomorrow." Hell, I'd come tonight. "I just need to call my sergeant and throw some stuff into a bag."

"No. He meant come home, come home. To Boston. To—"

"A real police department," I finished, trying to keep the bitterness out of my voice. I had heard the refrain so many times, I could finish my father's sentence for him.

Manny nodded.

My chest was so heavy and uncomfortable, I almost felt like I was having my own heart attack. "I can't."

"Why not? A couple years ago, you were talking like a move was imminent. Pops was even making inquiries in C-6 for you," he said, naming the district that served South Boston, where all the cops in my family—except me —had started their careers.

I sighed. "I'll come home for a visit, but I can't come back for good. Not yet."

"Why the hell not, Art? Come on. Playtime's over. Come home and make your old man happy. Be a real cop. What is it about this place that's got you so on the hook?"

I looked up. She was like a goddamned magnet.

And she was looking right at me.

DAWN

Apparently I wasn't the only one around campus with daddy issues. Though it seemed like Officer Perez's were kind of the opposite of mine. Whereas I couldn't get my father to give me the time of day for longer than it took to write a check, it sounded like my favorite campus cop's dad was all up in his face all the time.

I laughed to myself as I hurried out of the bar. Since when had I started thinking of Officer Unfriendly as my favorite cop? Since he rescued me from Royce's evil clutches? His take on that night was that I had been in the process of rescuing myself. And maybe I had, physically. But the way Officer Perez cut right through my borderline hysterics, the way he gathered up all the fleeing pieces of my self and smooshed them back together with those three little words: *I see you...* Well, eight months later, it still made me shiver.

"Officer Perez!" He was about half a block ahead of me, and I broke into a jog to catch up. He stopped when he heard me and turned. It was so strange to see him in normal clothes. Strange and...affecting. He wasn't wearing anything remarkable, just jeans and a plain white shirt T-shirt. Like his cop shirts, it was tight. I'm sure it was an XL, but *those arms*. The poor shirt wasn't up to the task of containing them, and his bulging muscles stretched the fabric taut.

I wasn't sure what to say as I approached him. I hadn't thought this out beyond bailing from my confab in the bar and coming after him, and now I felt weird. He was wearing an unreadable expression, and I was huffing a little from my jog. But who was I kidding? That's not why

48

I felt weird. I felt weird because the last time we were alone together, I kissed him.

I felt weird because I wanted to do it again.

"I, ah, couldn't help but overhear in there. I wanted to say that I'm sorry. About your dad." It was the truth. Seeing him so broken up in there had been strange. And the way his brother kept getting on his case had made me want to jump to his defense, to tell this Manny guy that his brother was doing good, important things at Allenhurst.

He kept staring at me with an even, inscrutable expression. It was maddening. I wanted him to say something.

"Thanks," he finally said.

"I was, ah, thinking maybe I could drive you home." I adjusted the straps of my backpack. "You know, because of all those times you've taken me home after bad stuff has gone down?" It sounded stupid when I said it like that, but I was seized with the need to make sure that he got home okay. That *he* was okay. "My car is around the corner, and I barely had anything to drink at the bar."

To my surprise, he smiled. "I walked. I'm only a few blocks from here."

"Oh." I had always imagined him living farther from campus. Or, let's not pretend—really, I had imagined him living in a magical mountain where he watched campus happenings from on high.

"But you can walk with me if you like." He reached for my backpack. It was super full because I'd had a big day with three classes, an editing session with Jenny, and my meeting in the bar, all with no time for stops at home in between. "But let me carry this."

"I can carry it, I—"

He tugged it out of my grip and slung it over one shoulder like it was nothing.

I sighed. I actually audibly sighed. Was I officially perving on Officer Perez now? I'd tried to tell myself that ill-advised kiss last winter was because I was all discombobulated and out of sorts. It had been a weird, organic reaction to a stressful situation, I'd assured myself. But really, I think, I had just wanted to do it. I saw my chance, and I took it. And I'd been thinking about it ever since, about the way he had simply sat there and let me. There had been a kind of harnessed strength in him, like there was a snake coiled inside his chest that was more powerful than anything I could dish out.

Dang it, I *was* perving on him.

"What were you doing in that bar?" he asked after we'd covered a couple blocks in silence.

"I told you, I'm legal now!" I protested. "I was just having a drink—"

"But you hadn't actually drunk any of your drink," he pointed out. The street we were on was full of large houses subdivided into student apartments, but they were gradually giving way to tidy bungalows that looked like they were occupied by regular people. "Your friend had nearly finished hers. Were you working?"

"I wasn't *working*. I was—"

"Do you ever turn off the inner gossip? That's what I'm asking." He stopped walking and turned, squinting at me under the yellow glare of a streetlight. "Can you live without constantly building your so-called social power?"

The way he said "social power" made me uncomfortable. A lot of what I said or thought sounded wrong when he repeated it back to me. Seeing myself through his eyes was unsettling.

"Do you ever go out to have a drink with someone just to have a drink with someone?" he asked, since I hadn't answered his previous questions.

"Is that an invitation?" I asked, though I couldn't believe I had the guts.

"Would I show up in Dish with Dawn tomorrow if it was?" he countered right away, almost like he was angry, and started to walk again, faster this time.

"Of course not."

He sighed, slowing to let me catch up with him. "You do a lot of good work with that column, but I'm not sure it's serving you."

I blinked, struggling to adjust to the change of topic. I'd thought for a minute he was asking me out, but apparently not. But then my brain stalled on "You do a lot of good work with that column." As with the time I'd seen him at parent orientation, I was too pleased by his praise.

"It's only a silly gossip column," I said, seized with the need to deflect the compliment, perhaps because I *was* so pleased by it.

"Sometimes. But take that football scandal. You can't say justice wasn't served there."

"Wow. Justice served. Coming from a cop, that's saying something." I was still trying to downplay what he was saying, but I wasn't sure why, because I was super proud of that story.

"It's a different kind of justice. That's what I'm saying. You did something we couldn't have. None of those girls ever came forward to talk to police. We had no idea that was going on. You keep saying that your column isn't important. If you believe that, why do you do it? What drives you? Are you going to be a journalist?"

"No." Jenny was always asking me that, too, telling me

I had talent and pointing out that because of my father, I'd have my pick of plum jobs after I graduated. But I wasn't interested in journalism, not really. The column had started for shallow reasons and had grown into something I was proud of, but it wasn't what I wanted to do with my whole life. "I think I want to be a psychologist or a counselor of some sort," I said, voicing the desire aloud for the first time. "I think people are fascinating." I paused, unsure how to explain. "I just don't think…"

"You don't think what?" He looked at me while we walked, his eyes drilling into mine.

I don't think I'm smart enough. I don't know why anyone should trust me to help them sort out their problems. But I didn't say that, because I knew, somehow, that it would anger him. My face flushed, and I broke with his gaze, no longer able to withstand his scrutiny.

But he kept pressing, even though I kept staring at the pavement passing beneath my feet. "So you don't think the column is important, and it isn't related to your chosen career path. Here's my question, then: Is it worth it?"

"What do you mean?"

"You're always with people—you're at the center of everything—but you're always alone."

I heard my sharp inhale of breath. "I have a huge story coming out next week," I snapped. It was the truth. I finally had Professor Daniels. I had a girl who had spoken to me anonymously about being blackmailed to provide sexual favors in return for grades, and her roommate had been able to corroborate her story. Jenny had the story lawyered, and we were ready to go for the last edition before summer break. By the time I left to go home for the summer, it was going to be huge news.

He smiled weakly and shook his head as he started walking again. "Well, good luck with that."

I was annoyed. I'd come after him to see if he was okay, to say I was sorry about his dad, and now I was somehow on the defensive?

"This is me." He stopped in front of one of the bunga-lows, a small, yellow-brick thing surrounded by a tidy lawn and a pretty flower garden.

Was he going to ask me in? Was that what that comment about having a drink had meant?

"I'm going to drive you back to your car."

Apparently not. But also, how typical was that of him? I walk him home, but then he has to drive me back to my car? I knew enough to know that arguing was futile. There was an Allenhurst PD squad car parked out in front of his house, so I got in and let him drive me the few blocks back to the bar. We didn't speak until he turned and said, "I'm not going to be around the next couple weeks, I don't think. So have a great summer."

CHAPTER SIX

The *Allenhurst Examiner*, May 29, 1983, Page 1A

Dish with Dawn – Special Report

**COMMUNICATION PROFESSOR BRIBES STUDENT:
SEX IN EXCHANGE FOR AN A**

[Editor's note: Those of you who follow Dish with Dawn in its usual spot on the back page of the paper will have noticed a series of blind items over the past year alluding to an unnamed professor preying on students by offering them academic outcomes in return for sexual favors. Blind items have long been a staple in the world of gossip. A blind item is a piece of news that is reported without revealing the identity of the individuals involved. Sometimes that identity is withheld out of fear of lawsuits. In other cases, as with Dawn's recent blind items, the basics of the story were known but the identities of the individuals involved were not. We now know the identities of the parties in question, and what was gossip has become news.

The story reported here has been verified by two independent sources, both of whom asked that their names be withheld. We have given them pseudonyms for the purposes of this story. Dawn has retained her conversational style of writing, but all the highest standards of ethical journalism have been employed in the reporting of this story.]

The first time it happened, Pamela was a little bit flattered. She's embarrassed by that sentiment now, but she's committed to telling the truth about what happened between her and Professor Gary Daniels of the Department of Communication.

"I was taking Intro to Media Studies," says the sophomore. "I'd recently decided to switch majors. I was catching up on some of the intro classes in communication, so I was a year older than most of the other students."

Pamela had been a sociology student prior to switching to communication, and when asked why she made the switch, she blushes and admits that she was kicked out of sociology because her GPA was too low. "I needed to salvage my college career, to be honest. I come from a conservative, old-fashioned family. I can't disappoint my parents. Flunking out of college would shame them. So my plan was to double down and take extra courses to make up for declaring comm so late and try to catch up. I figured I'd still need to do an extra semester, but at least I had a plan."

One afternoon, Pamela stopped by Daniels's office to ask some questions about an assignment she was struggling with. "He locked the door behind me," she says, visibly upset over the memory. "And then he kissed me. There was no lead-in. He just kissed me."

Pamela reports that Daniels then undertook a campaign of flattery, telling her she was so much prettier and more mature than the other students, that he couldn't help himself. What followed was an escalating series of sexually charged banter and several heavy-petting sessions.

Then Pamela tried to break things off. "It was tearing me up inside. On the one hand, I was flattered that this smart, older guy was so into me. But I knew it was wrong. I kept hearing my mother's voice in my head. That wasn't how I was raised. Also, I was struggling in several of my classes, including his, and I felt like the whole thing was distracting me from my studies. I asked him if he would wait until I was done with college for anything more to happen between us." She shakes her head and angrily swipes away tears. "I was so stupid."

At that point, Daniels laid down an ultimatum. Pamela was on her way to failing his class. If she had sex with him once, she'd get a C. If she had sex with him on demand throughout the semester, she'd get an A.

"I figured an A would go a long way toward upping my GPA by balancing some of my less bitchin' grades. And if I was going to do it once..." She chokes up, as she does several times during our interview. "I am such a ditz. That wasn't how I was raised," she says, using a phrase that comes up numerous times during our time together.

Despite her misgivings, Pamela agreed to Daniels's demand, and the two began having sex, usually in his office, but sometimes in his apartment and once in his car. She thought she was handling it but was surprised when her roommate forced an intervention.

Pamela's roommate Kathleen agreed to speak to me, too, separately from Pamela.

"I could tell something was wrong with her, but I

didn't know what it was," Kathleen says. "She wasn't eating. She wasn't usually much of a drinker, at least not outside of organized parties. But then she started bringing home these bottles of wine, and she'd drink one almost every night. Pamela comes from a really traditional family —they're big into church and all that. To be honest, she was kind of a goody-goody her first year here, so I thought maybe she was letting loose a little, you know? Shaking off the chains of her background or something. But then she started drinking a bottle of wine *before* she went out for the evening. She'd leave stumbling and slurring her way out the door to study sessions—and there were *a lot* of study sessions all of a sudden."

Kathleen confronted Pamela, expecting that she was forcing the issue on an eating disorder or an addiction.

"I had no idea that these behaviors were about coping with what was really going on."

Kathleen encouraged Pamela to go to the police, but Pamela was still committed to "earning" her A. She was also terrified of anyone finding out.

"It sounds ridiculous now," Pamela says, "but by the time I told Kathleen what was going on, the semester was two-thirds over. I felt like I was so close. But, really, the biggest deterrent was the idea of my family finding out. They would never get over it. They would…" She trails off, clearly fighting tears. "I don't even know what they would do."

What was the event that finally pushed Pamela to talk to the *Examiner*?

"I walked in on him having sex with another girl," she says. Her previously tearful demeanor turns angry. "It turned out that after everything, somewhere deep inside, I still thought I meant something to him. I knew I was going against every moral I was raised with, I knew I was disappointing my family and God, but I guess I thought…it was okay if he loved me."

Pamela did briefly consider going to the police then. With Kathleen's help, she even recorded a conversation with Daniels. She ultimately balked at taking it to police, though.

"I couldn't do that to my family. They would never be able to forgive me. They'd be shunned, kicked out of our church. They would have to move."

Pamela allowed me to listen to the tape once, though she would not let me make a copy or transcribe it. It contains a conversation between a Pamela and a man who answers Pamela's greeting of "Professor Daniels." In the recording, she confronts him about the other girl she'd caught him with, and he tells her she's overreacting. The tape is short, and the recording stops after the man tells Pamela, "You'll get your A."

Pamela did get the A.

"But," she says, "I didn't think he should be allowed to keep doing this. So…here I am."

The *Boston Voice*, July 15, 1983

Regional News, Page 2B

ALLENHURST STUDENT TAKES OWN LIFE AFTER SEX BRIBERY SCANDAL

Julianne Lansing, a twenty-year-old student at Allenhurst College who had recently accused Professor Gary Daniels of the college's communication department of offering her favorable grades in exchange for sex, has been found dead in her off-campus apartment of an apparent drug overdose, though a medical examiner has yet to rule.

Lansing, using the alias "Pamela," told her story to the campus newspaper's gossip columnist, Dawn Hathaway, and the resultant article, published on May 29 in the *Allenhurst Examiner*, rocked the campus. Lansing, who was failing the Introduction to Media Studies course she was taking from Daniels, claimed that Daniels offered her a C to have sex with him once and an A in exchange for sex on demand.

The college immediately opened an investigation. Daniels claimed the story was fabricated, though Hathaway reported that she had listened to a tape Lansing made of Daniels referencing the end of his sexual relationship with the student.

In the *Examiner* story, Lansing repeatedly referenced a conservative, churchgoing family who would be devastated to learn of her behavior and cited her family as the reason she never went to police with her allegations.

"I had been encouraging her to go to the police," says Lansing's roommate, who was also given a pseudonym in the original article but later self-identified as Jill Jenkins and has been speaking to media in what she calls "an attempt to set the record straight."

"Julianne did nothing wrong," Jenkins insists, "other than cross paths with a heartless narcissist. She couldn't bring herself to go to police, but she thought that by talking to the campus newspaper—she knew and trusted the writer—she might be able to prevent him from doing this to other girls."

Lansing told the *Examiner* that her relationship with

Daniels ended when she caught him engaged in sex with another student.

"That caused her to see that this was bigger than her," says Jenkins. "She thought she was doing a good thing by telling her story, but it ended up killing her."

Jenkins reports that Lansing's worst fears were realized when the district attorney's office brought charges against Daniels independent of Lansing's cooperation. "She didn't understand that the state could bring charges on its own," said Jenkins. "Neither of us did."

Jenkins accompanied Lansing on a trip home to suburban Baltimore the weekend after the charges were brought against Daniels and Lansing's identity was revealed. The pair traveled eight hours by bus in the hopes of explaining things to Lansing's family in person.

"They wouldn't even let her in the house," says Jenkins. "The last thing she said to me was how much she regretted doing the interview with the *Examiner*."

Dawn Hathaway, gossip columnist at the *Examiner* and daughter of media titan Edward Hathaway, could not be reached for comment.

CHAPTER SEVEN

September 1983

ARTURO

I had been hoping to catch her alone before I saw her out and about that first week back. Most of the students came back sometime the first week of September, the week before classes started, and I didn't like the idea of seeing her at a party—seeing her "on the job," so to speak.

Hell, that wasn't right. "Hoping to catch her alone" made it sound like I was casually keeping my eyes peeled as I went about my business. That wasn't it at all.

The truth was, I had been *consumed* all summer with everything that had happened. With anxiety over how she was doing.

The article ran when I was off, back in Boston sharing angioplasty recovery duty with my mom and brother and sisters. I'd thought I had it bad, marinating as I was in guilt that not only had I not been there with everyone else when my dad had his attack, but that I was perpetually disappointing him by holding out at Allenhurst.

To make matters worse, he didn't ride me about it like he usually did. Even as he regained strength and went back to being his usual wisecracking self, he said nothing about my employment status. It was like he'd...given up, like I'd disappointed him so irrevocably that he'd washed his hands of me. That was somehow worse than all the years of nagging.

But then, the article. Dawn's article. Dawn's glorious, righteous shit-storm of an article. Talk about speaking truth to power. When Fuller called my folks' place to read it to me over the phone, it was all I could do not to whoop and fist-pump right there in the living room on Bowen Street.

She downplayed herself. She was in it for social power, she'd said. And maybe she had been initially. Hell, maybe she still was, but she couldn't ignore the *real* power her words had. Power for good. Power to put away that fucking Daniels predator. As I told Fuller, she was doing our job better than we were. I felt terrible for having told her the column wasn't worth it when I'd last seen her. Even if she didn't want to be a journalist, what she was doing was important.

Fuller told me that the Allenhurst city force was working with the DA's office, and that they were cooperating as needed but that there wasn't much to do but wait for the arraignment. I thought it best anyway, that whatever role the campus was playing, I stay at arm's length because of my...involvement with Dawn. Of course, I didn't tell that to Fuller. I merely asked the chief for another couple weeks off, using Dad as my excuse, and since it was summer and I rarely took any vacation, my request was granted.

Then Julianne killed herself.

Dawn wasn't on campus when I got back. I wasn't sure if she had been planning all along to be home for the summer, or if she'd turned tail—not that I would have blamed her—when tragedy struck. Regardless, when I got back to campus, her apartment was empty, and it remained so the rest of the summer. In addition to keeping my outdoor vigil, I'd gone up and knocked on her door several times, eventually running into a neighbor who filled me in on what was happening. Dawn was away, she'd reported, but was supposedly coming back in the fall.

And now it was fall. And I was losing my mind a little bit.

I looked for her in all the likely places, with no luck. I started to wonder if maybe she wasn't coming back to school at all.

But then I spotted her, in public.

It was at the orientation week barbecue, a giant blowout held on the campus's central quad on the Sunday afternoon before classes started. The huge lawn was taken over by tables staffed by all the campus clubs, their members selling burgers and brownies and trying to recruit freshmen. Though the event was targeted at new students, pretty much everyone on campus turned out for what functioned as the unofficial kickoff to the new school year. The campus police department always sent representatives, too, both because it was good to get a handle on the new crowd, but also because the event often spilled over into low-level trouble, with bands of drunk kids, reunited after their summers away, roaming around like trouble-magnets.

I was strolling the quad with Fuller when I saw her. She clearly wasn't "at" the event, though. She was trying to walk through it, and she put me in mind of a movie star trying to avoid attention. She had on a huge pair of wraparound sunglasses and wore a scarf over her head like Jackie O. She walked quickly, or at least as quickly as she could, given that the quad was jammed. There was a purposefulness to her stride that made my heart twist. Normally, she'd be at the center of an event like this, working the crowd, smiling and laughing, the queen bee cementing her "social power." Now she was hiding. And Dawn Hathaway hiding was…not right.

"I'll be right back," I said to Fuller, who nodded absently as he eyed a group of football players whipping a small crowd into a frenzy with some kind of chant.

I took off in the direction Dawn had been going, threading my way through the throng, struggling to keep her veiled head in my sights. People got out of my way, though—one of the perks of the job—and I began closing the gap.

The dynamics of a crowd can shift in the blink of an eye. It's part of why we always attend events like this one. There's a kind of mass psychology at work in crowds. What starts off as a benign, happy group of people can quickly turn into a sinister mob. You learn to look for the signs: alcohol, a common enemy, like in riots after a loss in a sporting event. But in some cases, there's no real cause. There's just a bunch of kids looking for an excuse to turn mean.

It started as whispers. I couldn't initially make them out, but as I approached, I could tell that they were purposeful, directed at something—or someone.

"…might as well be a murderer…thought she was above everyone else…"

I reared back almost as if one of the kids had physically hit me. Was that how this was playing out on campus? I'd been sick with worry for Dawn because I was afraid she was going to blame herself, but it had never occurred to me that everyone else would too.

I had to get to her. Her head was down, and she was trying to push through the increasingly hostile scrum.

"Two-faced bitch!" someone yelled.

"Are you happy now?" came another jeer.

"You think you're the fucking queen of this campus, don't you?"

She stopped, and so did I. Whirling, she removed her sunglasses and ripped off her headscarf, as if she had decided to face her accusers head-on. Her usually fluffy hair was flat, stringy, and her face was gaunt, pale. I realized I'd never seen her without her signature brightly colored eye shadow. She looked so utterly unlike herself, I was shocked. I think everyone else was too, because the crowd instantly shut up.

"No," she said, her voice quiet but strong. "No, I'm not happy." She swiped angrily at her face, as if to wipe away tears, but there weren't any there. "Anything else?" she asked as she surveyed the assembly.

The mob stayed silent, utterly riveted by her. It was like she was the conductor in *Fantasia*, controlling the scene before her.

Her bravery took my breath away.

She turned then and continued on her journey. Those shitheads weren't wrong, in a way, for calling her a queen, because it *did* feel like she was dismissing her subjects. But suddenly, as if she'd thought better of it, she stopped walking and turned back to them—no, to me. Her eyes found mine instantly, latched onto my gaze like a heat-seeking missile.

Our eyes were connected, but for a moment, I felt like our bodies were, too. Because my throat ached with the tears she wasn't shedding, as if her grief was mine.

Then she broke eye contact, shoved her sunglasses back on, and took off.

DAWN

Coming back had been a mistake. I should have done what Daddy said and transferred somewhere closer to home. I could easily have finished my degree at the City University of New York. Yeah, it might have meant an extra year because not all my credits would have transferred cleanly, but what was an extra year in the scheme of things? I had nothing but years. I had my whole damn life ahead of me.

And now that I wasn't taking that fact for granted anymore, I didn't know how to be. Because there wasn't anything left. Underneath all that entitlement I'd worn around for so many years like a heavy cloak, there was…nothing.

"I should go back," I'd told my father, even as it wasn't lost on me that he and I were having the longest face-to-face conversation I could ever remember. Ironically, I'd finally—unintentionally—done something big enough to earn his sustained attention. "I only have five more required classes." I had sketched out a plan, which I showed him, to cram all the remaining credits for my psych degree into the fall semester. It was going to be intense, but I could graduate in December.

He had nodded and agreed and, to my utter shock, suggested that I consider doing a master's degree in journalism after I graduated. I'd shown a ruthlessness he hadn't known I'd possessed, he'd said. Maybe I was cut out to follow in his footsteps after all. Stunned, I'd told him I would consider it. And I was. I couldn't get into the best journalism schools with my mediocre grades, but once I had that master's in hand, what did it matter which school it came from? Maybe my father was right. Maybe Jenny was right. I did seem to be good at getting people to talk to me, to tell me their secrets. Journalism didn't feel like the best fit, but what did I know? I had all these smarter, more accomplished people telling me I could do it. I had my *father* telling me I could do it, which felt like I was starving and he'd placed a feast in front of me.

Anyway, regardless of what came after graduation, I was, at my own insistence, going to be at Allenhurst for the next few months. And as I'd sketched out my plans for my father, I hadn't told him the truth about why. I hadn't told *anyone* the truth, which was that coming back was my penance.

I could crawl home to Daddy's penthouse and get lost at CUNY, where no one knew my name, or I could come back to Allenhurst and face the truth. I had chosen the latter. I came back so they could say it to my face, because that was what I deserved.

Murderer.

But I was crumbling. I had dragged myself back, but it turned out I wasn't strong enough to face the consequences of my actions. I'd been back three days; school hadn't even started yet. I was never going to survive.

It wasn't so much what other people were saying. For the first time in my life, I honestly didn't give a shit what other people said about me. It was the idea that *she* wasn't here. That Julianne, with whom I'd had a friendly acquaintanceship before our interview, would never again attend an orientation barbecue on the quad. That she couldn't switch majors yet again and have the chance to fix her GPA. That she would never be with a guy who was worthy of her.

And that it was all my fault. I'd been so wrapped up in the idea of the column, of a big, juicy story to cement my power and popularity, that I hadn't really thought about what I was saying. About what that power I had so craved could do. "Is it worth it?" Officer Perez had asked me once. I'd scoffed at him.

If only I had listened.

But maybe Daddy was right. Maybe leveraging the explosive story into a career in journalism would make it worth it. Would redeem me somehow.

I shrieked when there was a knock at the door.

This happened now. I'd get so lost in my thoughts, in reliving everything, that I'd completely forget about my surroundings. Consequently, I was always jumpy. Always on edge. Perpetually ready for fight or flight, though I could do neither. It only took the smallest thing to set me off, to send a raging, poisonous river of adrenaline coursing through me.

It was probably Beth, the new editor of the paper since Jenny had graduated. Beth had been trying to get me to come back to the *Examiner*—yet another foot soldier in the battle to convert me into a journalist. Her persistence would have made me laugh if laughing was something I still did. She'd been calling and calling, saying I had the makings of a totally boss investigative journalist, and in her last message, she'd threatened to come over to my apartment. I was tempted to pretend not to be home, but if Beth was anything like her predecessor, she wouldn't give up until I made her understand that whatever I decided about my future career path, even if I *did* decide to pursue journalism, I was never, ever coming back to the *Allenhurst Examiner*. Dish with Dawn was dead. Forever. Because the Dawn who'd written it was too.

The knocking grew more insistent. I shuffled to the door on legs that felt made of cement.

It was him.

Officer Perez. Officer Artie. Officer Unfriendly. He wasn't in uniform. Well, he was wearing faded jeans and a T-shirt, which seemed to be his off-duty uniform. The T-shirt this time was pale pink, which set off his light brown skin, but it was as tight as the one he'd worn in the bar last time I saw him, a lifetime ago, back when I was a different person. Back when I'd dismissed him when he tried to caution me about the dangerous game I was playing.

He just stood there, looking at me with those gorgeous eyes, eyes that, remarkably, seemed to be shining with something like compassion.

"What's your name?" I asked. "Your first name." I wanted to know, suddenly. Jenny had always called him Artie, but surely that wasn't his actual given name.

"Arturo," he said. "My name is Arturo Perez."

"How old are you?" I asked. I don't know why I cared so much about all these details. All I could think was that I had never paid attention to details about him before, or at least I'd paid attention to the wrong ones. I'd catalogued his green-flecked brown eyes, for example, but I'd never seen the compassion in them.

He furrowed his brow. "Thirty-one."

"I'm twenty-two," I said, because it felt like the logical next line in the conversation.

"I know." When I didn't answer, he shot me a lopsided grin and added, "I've written you a ticket or two in my day. I've seen your ID."

My brain knew he was teasing. Making a joke. My brain also knew that what people did in response to jokes was laugh. But it was like my mouth didn't know how to do it.

I watched his face for clues about what should happen next, and when his eyebrows shot up, I followed his gaze to my body—my body, which was covered by the leather jacket he had given me that night after Royce attacked me at the Delta Chi party. I'd worn it around the house pretty much all the time in the days following that event. It was big and heavy. It had comforted me then, and it did now, too. Its weight anchored me in place, made me feel like maybe I wouldn't simply dissolve and float away in my grief.

Probably I should be embarrassed, my mind told me, because I was wearing the jacket, but also because I was only wearing a T-shirt and panties beneath it. Instead, my mouth said, "I have your windbreaker, too." It was true. I had a veritable collection of Allenhurst Campus PD outerwear.

Instead of commenting on the jackets, he said, "Your heart is broken," because, somehow, he knew.

Four words. Four little words, but it was like they had chiseled a hairline fracture in the invisible shellac that surrounded me, and the air in my lungs was hissing out of that crack. But I guess it shouldn't have been so surprising that his words had such power. Words had power. I understood that now.

It was becoming harder and harder to breathe, but I managed to answer him anyway. "Not broken. Just gone. It's like my heart…just isn't there."

"No." He shook his head almost violently, like he was trying to forget something unpleasant he had seen. "It's there. You can't see it right now. But it's there, I promise you. There's something in the way—something blocking your sense of it, but it won't be in the way forever."

The tiny crack he'd chiseled into me opened up then, all at once, into a gaping canyon. It was like my organs, which had been squished together in a familiar, tight jumble, were violently ripped apart and exposed to the cold air, left writhing, blinking in the light like baby birds tipped prematurely out of their nests.

And it hurt. It was fucking excruciating. I felt it almost literally, like an actual chasm was opening up inside me.

But then his arms were around me, putting me back together, and he was saying, "It's okay. Go ahead and cry."

Was I crying?

I must have been operating in a vacuum, where sound had been muffled, because all of a sudden it was like someone turned on the sound in what had been a silent movie. My sobs rang out across the apartment and through the hallway, since we were standing in the doorway to my place.

I couldn't move, though, and I couldn't stop. My brain kept going over the images that had been cycling through it on an endless loop all summer: Julianne and Jill, coming to the *Examiner* offices late that night, both of them serious, looking older than their years. Julianne's face as she described Daniels's advances. And then the loop veered off reality and sped through pictures I could only imagine: Julianne's lifeless face as she lay on the floor—Beth, who had reported on the suicide for the *Allenhurst Examiner*, had talked to the cops and learned that she'd been found on the floor of her bedroom by her roommate, a detail that had been kept out of the initial news reports. Jill's face when she found Julianne cold and dead.

I'd been seeing those images; they weren't new. But now I was really *seeing* them. The color was turned up, the sound was turned up—*everything* was turned up.

My sobs grew louder, more anguished. It was almost like they were coming from outside my body. I could feel my chest heaving, but at the same time, it was like it was happening to someone else. I could hear myself becoming more and more unhinged, but I couldn't do anything about it.

Officer Perez could, though. *Arturo* could. He held me tight me as I cried. Those arms I'd perved out over for so many years… It was like they were containing everything inside me that was trying to fly away. They were strong, but patient.

They reminded me of the only other time someone had taken that much care with me. And of course, that would have been the only other time I stood inside Arturo's embrace, that night Royce was on his coke binge and I became uncharacteristically hysterical.

"I see you," he'd said that night. I thought he'd meant right then. Like he was saying it to snap me out of that weird, scary fight-or-flight mode I'd been in.

But maybe he really did. Really, truly did.

The thought was shocking enough to make me stop crying.

Intriguing enough to make me pull back against those

steadfast arms, which immediately loosened their grip but did not fully release me.

Compelling enough to let my hands float up and come to rest on his cheeks, which were dusted with the stubble of late afternoon.

I kept expecting him to stop me, to push me away like he had last time, in his car after that disaster of a Delta Chi party. To say that my defenses were down, that my judgment was clouded by my emotional state.

It was true. But it wasn't all of the truth. The truth was, I wanted to be seen. No, I wanted *him* to see me. No, not even that. The hard kernel of truth I carried around deep inside was that I just wanted *him*.

"This is not a good idea," he murmured before my lips hit his.

"You're not thinking clearly," he rasped as I let go of his cheeks and snaked my arms around his neck.

"*I'm* not thinking clearly," he whispered as I hitched myself up, holding onto his neck for leverage as I wrapped my legs around his waist.

He caught me. Kept me.

Kissed me.

He licked deep into my mouth, stroking me with a tongue that was insistent but unhurried, which should have been a contradiction but somehow wasn't.

I hadn't had a boyfriend since high school. There had been a couple casual, short relationships the first semester of freshman year at Allenhurst, but once I started the column, I'd eschewed boys entirely. They kept me too busy to do the socializing necessary to make and maintain my connections. Still, between high school and those early college encounters, I'd had my share of kisses.

This was not like those kisses. The boys I'd kissed

before had always made me feel like kissing was a prelude to something else. Something to get out of the way so other, bigger, more important things could happen. They might not have meant it that way, but there was an undercurrent of impatience that I could usually sense, like their desire was too big to be kept at bay for very long.

Arturo's desire was big. I didn't mean that literally, but it was that, too. I could feel him, thick and hard, between my legs, the heavy denim of his jeans not sufficient to contain him. But it was also controlled. He pressed against my now-wet panties but not in a demanding way, not like he was trying to move things along, more like it simply felt good. I got the feeling that he could stand there forever, supporting my full body weight and kissing me. Like he *wanted* to stand there forever. Like kissing me was enough. Like I, right now, as wretched as I was, was enough.

But of course it couldn't last. He was too good. I could only be happy that it lasted as long as it did—that it happened at all—before he set me down. He tried to, anyway. He broke our kiss with a gasp and loosened his grip on me, but since I had all four limbs wrapped around him like a koala bear hugging a tree, nothing happened.

He laughed, which was pretty much the last thing I would have expected, and his arms came back around me and he carried me inside my apartment, kicking the door shut with his foot. He walked clear across my living room until he was standing over my sofa, then tried to dislodge me again. I had to let him. It would have been too embarrassing not to.

"Don't make a big speech about how that was a mistake," I said.

"Okay."

"Okay?" I echoed. I had braced myself for an onslaught of recriminations and regrets.

"Well, it was, but I won't make the speech if you don't want me to."

I blinked, stunned into silence by his agreeableness.

"You have classes tomorrow?"

It all came back, rushing at me like a roaring river—where I was, who I was, *what* I was. It was like I'd been fighting to swim against the current, like some stupid, doomed salmon, and kissing Officer Perez had taken me out of that current for a moment, for long enough to get my breath—for long enough to forget.

But it was almost worse, having had that reprieve, to be plunged back into the cold, black, relentless water.

"Your classes," he was saying, over-enunciating and stooping so he could get his face right close to mine. "What time are they over tomorrow?"

"Four," I said.

He stepped back with a small smile, as if my answer pleased him. "I'm on the seven-to-three shift tomorrow, so that's perfect."

"Perfect for what?"

"What building is your last class in?" he asked, ignoring my question in favor of posing his own.

"Stanton Hall," I answered.

"I'll pick you up outside Stanton at five past four," he said. He glanced at the floor. No, at my feet, actually, which, like my legs, were bare. I wanted to wiggle my toes under his scrutiny, but I forced myself to be still. "Wear comfortable shoes."

"Is this a...date?" I asked, bewildered.

"Nope," he said. Then he put on his sunglasses and walked out the door.

CHAPTER EIGHT

ARTURO

When I pulled up in front of Stanton Hall, I no longer thought what I was doing was a mistake.

I'd driven home from Dawn's place yesterday afternoon and gotten immediately into a cold shower, whereupon I'd sifted through everything that was fucked up about the whole situation. I was nine years older than she was. I was an employee of the college, and she was a student. Worse, I was in a position of authority at the college where she was a student. True, I didn't have power over her academic future like that Daniels asshole had over Julianne's, but it was difficult to get more authoritative than "cop."

But in the end, I couldn't convince myself that any of it mattered enough to dissuade me. I hadn't gotten as far as I had in my career without having good instincts, and my instincts said today was going to be hell for Dawn. She was drowning, and she needed help. She needed a friend.

Despite her previous popularity, I didn't think she truly had any of those.

The emphasis needed to be on *friend*, though. I couldn't undo the past, but I could do my job, which was to look out for the people on this campus. Wasn't that why I was so stubbornly hanging on here despite all the family pressure to jump ship?

Except, I had to admit, I wasn't really here in the line of duty, as evidenced by the fact that I was driving my own car. Dawn was probably looking for the cruiser, because although I was parked less than half a block down from the main entrance to the building, idling on the side of the road, she didn't recognize my beat-up Camaro.

Her obliviousness gave me a few moments to watch her unobserved. My gut had been right. She looked like she'd been through the wringer. Her hair was back to its usual poufy state, so she'd clearly tried to armor herself for the day, but her eyes didn't lie. I'd flattered myself that some warmth had come back into them by the time I left her apartment yesterday, but they were back to being haunted. Hunted.

I pulled up closer to where she was standing and watched her eyes widen—anything was better than that haunted look—when she realized it was me. I leaned over and cranked down the window. "Hop in." She smiled almost shyly as she obeyed, which was weird, because I was pretty sure Dawn Hathaway didn't do shy. At least the old Dawn Hathaway hadn't. I wanted to pepper her with questions, but I held back, letting a surprisingly comfortable silence settle over us as I navigated away from campus and onto the highway. Allenhurst was a typical college town, a mini-metropolis full of students, hippies, and townsfolk. But it was remote—you didn't have to drive far from town to get to the country.

"So you're not, like, planning to abduct me or anything, I hope," she said, breaking the silence when I pulled off the interstate onto a rural two-lane highway.

"They kind of frown on cops abducting people, so I try not to make a habit of it," I said, still having to work to prevent myself from besieging her with questions. *What did people say to you today? Where did you eat lunch? Did anyone give you trouble? Tell me their names.* "Here we are." I pulled off the road to a little grass-covered clearing.

Dawn hopped out of the car and made her way to a sign that marked the entrance to the trail. "'Dunkirk Creek Trail'?" she read.

"Yep. It's a creek that runs through the countryside here. There's a right of way owned by the county, which maintains a public trail."

"We're going *hiking*?"

The incredulity in her tone and the way she scrunched up her nose were awfully cute. "We are." I let my eyes travel down her body to check that she was properly outfitted. She was wearing a black sweatshirt with raw seams, and light blue jeans tucked into black-and-white-striped legwarmers. She looked like an extra in a Pat Benatar video. Her outfit was capped off with pale pink high-top sneakers, which was the most important thing, given the uneven terrain we'd be tromping over.

But then, because I was a bastard, I let my eyes travel back up, taking in the same jeans and sweatshirt, but this time appreciating how they hugged her small, perfectly proportioned body. I'd felt those slight curves beneath my hands, pressed against my chest, flooding all my senses as

I'd held her yesterday, and I was having trouble turning off the reptilian part of my brain that was shouting "Again!"

Tamping down a wave of lust, I turned toward the entrance to the trail. "Come on."

"I haven't been hiking since I was a kid," she said as she fell into step behind me.

"Yeah, I guess New York City doesn't present a ton of hiking opportunities." I was gratified that she was talking. I'd learned from my dad that it was easier to talk when you were doing something, especially something that didn't require you to look at the other person. Hence the hike.

"Nope. But my father used to send me away to sleep-away camp upstate all summer when I was a kid."

Her choice of words—send me *away*—did not escape my attention. "So what's with this no-mother business?" It was a terribly personal question, but given the magnitude of the summer's events, I thought it might feel like less of a big deal to talk about, relatively speaking.

"My dad accidentally knocked up some woman he then paid off to have me and hand me over."

"Jesus." It took a lot to shock me. Allenhurst wasn't exactly a hotbed of crime, but you're a cop for long enough and you've pretty much seen the worst humanity has to offer.

"I'm exaggerating," she said, "but only a little. I used to have visits with her, but they stopped when I was thirteen. I asked if I could move in with her. She got all flustered, and then she wrote me a letter a couple weeks later saying it was better if we didn't see each other anymore. I can only assume my dad made that happen, and that he used his customary tool to do so—money."

"You never tried to reestablish contact?"

"Of course I did. I wrote and apologized, said I didn't

need to live with her. She just…never wrote back."

What she was saying was heartbreaking, but it was good that she was saying it. I'd had a feeling she had been living in her own head all summer. I'd wanted to get her talking about Julianne and the article, and her experience being back on campus, but I'd take what I could get. And I truly wanted to know where she had come from, was intensely curious about the circumstances that had shaped her.

"Your dad stayed single all this time?" I asked.

"No. He got married when I was twelve."

I didn't miss that that had been a year before she asked her mother if she could move in.

"That's when I started going to summer camp," she went on. "His wife didn't want me around over the summer."

"Oh, that can't be true," I protested. "Blended families are hard."

"It is true," she said matter-of-factly. "I overheard them talking about it. I went to a boarding school during the year, but she wanted me gone over the summer, too."

Shit. No wonder Dawn was so perpetually in search of popularity. After facing rejection after rejection as a child, she simply wanted to be wanted. When she'd talked about her father not seeing her, I'd assumed she'd meant it metaphorically. I think she had, but it seemed it was also literally true.

There was a fallen log in the path, so I jumped over it and held my hand out to help her over it.

Instead of taking it, she stopped and cocked her head, staring at me from the other side of the log. "Why are you being so nice to me?"

I wasn't easily flustered, but the question threw me,

perhaps because I didn't know how to answer it in a way that wasn't at least partly selfish.

Instead of pressing me to answer, she hopped up on the log, but rather than come down the other side of it, she grabbed my hand and started walking along it lengthwise, like a tightrope walker. The log slanted upward, so she got higher and higher, and soon I was reaching up in order to continue holding her hand.

"You can see the creek from up here," she said.

"Yeah. The trees are pretty thick on this section of the trail, but if we go about ten more minutes down it, we'll come to a clearing where you can get right up next to the water."

She shook her hand out of my grasp and turned so she was facing me, then lowered herself to sit on the log, swinging her dangling legs back and forth. "Why are you being so nice to me?" she asked again. "I've never done anything but cause you trouble."

"I like you," I said, gambling that the truth wouldn't get me into too much trouble.

"You like me, or you like making out with me?"

Both. "I like you," I said emphatically, because she needed to hear that. But when her face fell a little, I said, "I liked making out with you, too." But before she got the wrong idea, I hastily added, "*Liked*, past tense. Because everything about that was wrong."

"Really?" she asked, and for a moment she reminded me of the old Dawn, always pushing, forever trying to get a rise out of me.

"Yes. To begin with, I'm—oh, shit."

She had leaned back and begun slowly sliding down from her perch, but she was a good five feet up. I instinctively reached for her to try to help break her fall, and she did that clinging thing she'd done yesterday, like she was the firefighter and I was the pole.

"I don't really want to hear all that," she whispered, when we were eye to eye, and once again, I had no choice but to hold onto her, to will my body to be calm in the face of almost unendurable temptation.

"All what?"

"All the reasons this shouldn't happen. You're too old. You're a cop, blah, blah, blah. I told you yesterday I didn't want to hear that speech."

Her face was two inches from mine. Her *lips* were two inches from mine. Jesus Christ, it just about killed me, but I closed my eyes and said, "Blah, blah, blah: that's exactly it. You can't blah, blah, blah over everything that's wrong with this." I attempted to shake her loose, but she held tight. "Let go of me," I said, as gently as I could.

She obeyed—kind of. Like that day I'd busted her stealing Ace, she slid down my body. There was no way she could miss my raging boner.

And she didn't. As her belly slid down over it, she raised one eyebrow and licked her lips before saying, "Blah, blah, blah?"

I wasn't at all sure how I was going to get out of this, but then she granted me an unexpected reprieve. Her feet hit the ground, and she stepped away from me and said, "So let's see this creek."

After a few minutes of silent hiking, which I used to compose myself, I decided to just ask what I wanted to ask. "How are you handling things?"

She spun around—she'd been walking ahead of me. "How do you think?"

"I think not well." When she started to protest, I said, "You know I was at the barbecue yesterday afternoon. I saw you trying to walk across the quad. I heard what they called you."

"What?" she said, her attitude morphing into one of defiance. "Murderer? So? They weren't wrong."

"They *were* wrong," I snapped, though the rational part of me knew getting annoyed at her wasn't going to help.

She turned and resumed marching down the trail toward the creek. "Looks like a duck. Walks like a duck."

"You can't think this is your fault, Dawn," I said, trying to gentle my tone.

"What part of it isn't my fault, Arturo?"

I didn't miss that she'd called me by my first name. It pleased me more than it should have. "All of it isn't your fault. You wrote a true, thorough, *important* article. It impressed the hell out of me when I read it."

"Yeah, well, it also killed an innocent girl."

Arguing wasn't going to help. I'd brought her out here because I'd had a hunch she wasn't talking to anyone, and that she needed to. I disagreed—vehemently—with her interpretation, but I didn't need to harass her about it. She'd heard my point of view. "You should call me Art," I said. "That's what my friends call me. Only my mother calls me Arturo."

She paused for the tiniest instant in her walking, so slightly that I almost missed it. "So it's not Officer Perez anymore?"

"Not in this context." I prayed she wouldn't needle me about exactly what "this context" was, because then we'd be back to blah, blah, blah, and I wasn't really on the moral or logical high ground there.

Mercifully, she didn't say anything. After a few more minutes of walking, we emerged into a little clearing on the side of the trail where you could walk right to the edge of the creek. She did so, stooping and picking up a handful of rocks and throwing them into the water one at a time. I stood next to her, hoping that the natural scene might somehow prove soothing.

"What do you think it feels like to die?" she asked, her voice so low I could hardly hear her over the rushing of the creek.

"Oh, sweetheart," I said, my voice breaking a little, because I knew how much her heart was breaking, too.

"I mean, I think you should know, right? Being a cop? Have you killed anyone, like I have?"

God. Every word out of her mouth was a lance to my chest. "I haven't killed anyone," I said, forcing myself to ignore my impulse to argue with her some more about her supposed culpability in Julianne's death. "I've had a couple incidents in my career where I've been called to the scene where someone was already dead. One was a homeless guy who froze to death, the other a domestic violence situation." I didn't say that I remembered them both like they had happened yesterday, that they stayed with me pretty much all the time.

"Right." She turned and shot me a grin that was clearly forced. "Because you're here at Allenhurst College instead of where the real action is, in Boston." I knew she was referencing what she'd overheard between my brother and me that night at the Allenhurst Tap Room. "Why haven't you left yet?"

My first impulse was that there was no way I could tell her the truth. But as we stared at each other and the silence between us stretched out, growing tauter, I revised my original take on the situation. Sure, I could tell her some version of what I'd told Manny and my dad, that I liked it here. That I felt like this was my community, and I wanted to serve it. That was true. But that wasn't all of the truth, not since I'd crossed paths with Dawn, anyway. And maybe the real truth would help her, the same way me telling her "I see you," seemed to have that night at Delta Chi. Dawn seemed to think she was alone in the world, and given what she'd told me about her asshole parents, maybe she *had* been. But she wasn't now. So I took a deep breath and told the truth.

"Because I can't leave you here alone."

She inhaled sharply, and tears gathered at the corners of her eyes, but she smiled through them. "That can't make your family happy. They seem…important to you."

She had hit on the central dilemma of my existence, the stupid conflict that kept me awake at night. My first impulse was to toss off something casual, dismissive, but that would have been the height of hypocrisy given that I'd taken her out here in the hopes of getting her to talk— to really talk. I hadn't expected to have the tables turned. "They *are* important to me," I said, choosing my words carefully. "We didn't have a lot growing up. I mean, we were fine, but four kids and a wife on a cop's salary didn't exactly mean we were living large. And we stuck out because we were pretty much the only Latino family in an Irish neighborhood. So we were tight. We made our own fun. My parents were always saying 'family first.'"

I looked down at her. She was staring at me with a wistful expression. "That sounds…pretty gnarly, actually."

"Yeah, so I'm the one who's perpetually disappointing them, by being out here."

"Because it's so far from Boston or—"

"You heard me talking to my brother." She had the grace to look embarrassed. "It's the distance, but it's also that they don't respect what I do." I ran my fingers through my hair in frustration. "It's hard to explain. My grandfather was a security guard. He immigrated to Boston when he was in his twenties. His dream was for my father to join the Boston PD, and I guess my father expanded on that dream. My brother fell in line—and so did one of my sisters, which I think my dad considered an unexpected bonus—but I did my own thing. I got really interested in community policing when I was in school, but they think it's policing-lite. It embarrasses them, I think. They see it as a step backward for the family, somehow."

"It sounded like you were going to go back, when I overheard you at the bar."

"Yeah, well, I was. And I still will—eventually. After my dad's heart attack, I took a leave of absence and went home for a month. I even had a meeting with a someone in HR on the Boston force."

"So what happened?"

"Julianne killed herself, and I was afraid of what it was going to do to you," I said, knowing more truth was a risk. I didn't want her to get the wrong idea about what was possible between us, but I wanted her to know that she mattered—enough to inspire people to change their plans, anyway.

She turned to look at the water again, and if I wasn't mistaken, she blushed a little as she did so.

"We should turn back," I said, feeling like I'd accomplished what I set out to do.

She bit her lower lip, the way people do when they're trying not to smile. She'd only just turned and begun trudging back the way we'd come when she said, "Blah, blah, blah."

CHAPTER NINE

December 1983

DAWN

The semester had been awful. I began each day by getting up and going through the motions of getting ready, doing the minimum required to get myself clean and push myself out the door. I sometimes looked at my vast collection of makeup with wonder, as if I were an archaeologist from another planet. What was it for? How had any of these powders and paints mattered to the girl who used to slather herself with them?

I attended my classes, sitting in the back and not making eye contact with anyone. I was the first one out of every lecture hall. I finished most days back home in my apartment, crying. I would hold it together until I burst through my door, and then a day's worth of pent-up grief would come flooding out of me.

It was like I was drowning, except not. Because if you were drowning, eventually, I presumed, it would be over.

You'd succumb to your watery fate. That fall at Allenhurst, though, I kept flailing and gasping, my lungs perpetually on the verge of collapse, unable to get a grip on anything that might anchor me, much less pull me to shore, dry me off, and set me to rights.

Except that wasn't entirely true. There was an anchor, and his name was Arturo Perez. Art, he'd told me to call him.

He was constantly checking on me, and he wasn't even trying to be subtle about it. He must have figured out my class schedule, because he was almost always waiting for me after my Environmental Psych class on Tuesdays and Thursdays. He was on duty, so he never did more than walk with me to the student center, where I usually passed the time until my next class. But it was a welcome break in the day, a pause in the assault I was perpetually enduring. The other students had calmed down somewhat and were mostly leaving me alone. They looked at me funny, still, and no one spoke to me—or rather, I didn't speak to them. But no one was outright calling me a murderer anymore. The DA was proceeding with charges against Daniels—some other girls had come forward with their own, similar stories—and I had cooperated when they wanted to interview me about Julianne, but I would be out of here before anything got resolved.

I knew gossip. I knew how quickly people forgot things, their attention captured by something newer, shinier, more horrible. What I had less experience with was how long the voices in my own head were going to keep dogging me. The assault I was enduring was self-inflicted. And it felt like it would never stop.

But then Art would show up, and it would. Only for a while, only until he left me again, but the reprieve was always enough to restore me sufficiently that I could get through the next little stretch. Every time felt like a small miracle.

And God help me, I wanted more. More respite. More time with him. More *of* him. I understood all the reasons I shouldn't want that—all the stuff I'd previously glossed over with the "blah, blah, blah" shorthand. I'd always thought he was hot, but now I knew he was kind, too, and I couldn't help myself. He was the only thing that made me feel not bad. I began living for the times I'd see him, Tuesdays and Thursdays like clockwork, but he would also sometimes surprise me out of the blue. Judging by what he was wearing, sometimes he was on duty, and sometimes he wasn't. An example of the latter was one time I was leaving my apartment early one morning in November, heading for an eight o'clock class, when suddenly there he was, falling into step next to me, two coffees in hand, one of which he silently passed to me. As he walked me to class, I found myself telling him about a research paper I was working on for my History of Psychology class. I smiled when I told him it was about the treatment of PTSD from the 1970s onward. We both laughed because we both saw the irony in it. It felt so strange to be laughing.

"Did you know that most major police forces have psychologists on staff?" he'd asked me.

"Oh, so maybe I could go join the Boston PD," I'd teased. "Like, in place of you. Maybe you could tell your family that I'm the sacrificial lamb, and they'll lay off."

His low laughter had rung out across the empty sidewalks, and I'd been flooded with something that felt like pride. The idea that someone like me could make someone like him laugh was strangely, sharply sweet.

From there, we'd talked a little bit about my career

options. I'd chosen psychology as a major for the shallowest of reasons—I'd thought it would help me understand people and improve my gossip column. But there I was, telling him everything that I liked about it. "People are so interesting, and there are so many ways they can sabotage themselves."

"You seem to have a knack for figuring people out," he'd said.

"Yeah, well, I think I'm going to go the journalism route." I had pretty much decided to take my father's advice and go to journalism school after I finished my B.A. He kept saying that my story about Julianne would get me into some decent schools, and he'd promised to set me up with a job afterward.

"Why would you do that?" he'd asked, visibly puzzled. "You told me before that you didn't want to do journalism."

I could hardly tell him that I wanted to do something to make my father proud. Not that there was anything wrong with wanting a parent to be proud of you, but he knew me better than to accept that explanation at face value. I also couldn't tell him the other reason. I'd barely articulated it to myself, but was clinging to a vague sense that if I went into journalism, maybe next time I was presented with an opportunity like Julianne's story, I would…get things right. It sounded stupid even in my own head, so I settled for "I don't think I'm cut out for psychology. It's not a practical option for me."

He'd stopped then, right there on the sidewalk, and set his coffee on the pavement. Then he took me by the shoulders and looked into my eyes and said, "You don't have to be a journalist if you don't want to, Dawn. It's okay to want what you want. Don't let other people live your life for you—you're smarter than that."

I hadn't known what to say to that, except maybe that his idealism was all fine and good but no match for twenty-two years of life with my father. Or not even *with* him, but *near* him.

Regardless, when we reached my class and parted ways, I was astonished to realize that, other than as it related to my reasons for considering journalism, I hadn't thought about Julianne the whole time I'd been with him.

So, yeah, I had my respite, was the point, and it was named Arturo.

And I wanted more.

One Saturday in mid-December, I was rattling around my apartment, and honestly, I wasn't doing super well. Weekends were always hard. Whereas I'd always been a middling student before, this semester I was getting straight As because I filled my weekends with nonstop schoolwork. It meant less time for thinking. But now the semester proper was over. I had exams next week, and I was already over-prepared for them. I flipped on the TV for the evening news, just to hear some human voices.

There was going to be a total lunar eclipse beginning shortly after midnight, the anchor informed me. Growing up in New York City, I'd never gotten to see that kind of stuff. Not that I'd cared back then, but...I wasn't the same person anymore, was I?

I hoofed it into the bathroom and threw on some mascara and lipstick, grabbed my coat, raced down the stairs, and pushed my way out the front door of my building. Gulping lungfuls of the cold, fresh air, I tilted my head back and scanned the sky until I found the big yellow grapefruit of a moon.

I glanced at my watch. It was late. It was crossing a line. More blah, blah, blahs. But I didn't care. The minute the anchor had said the words *total eclipse*, my mind had jumped back to that time he had come to my apartment. The words he had said to me then were still burned into my brain. "It's there. You just can't see it right now. But it's there, I promise you. There's something in the way— something blocking your sense of it, but it won't be in the way forever."

We hadn't been talking about the moon, of course. We'd been talking about my heart.

I didn't even go back upstairs for the car keys I'd forgotten to grab. I could do nothing that might make me lose my nerve. I just started walking.

ARTURO

The doorbell rang at eleven-thirty on Saturday night, and my first thought was that it was Manny. Which was ridiculous, because I had spoken to my parents on the phone earlier in the evening and everything was fine—fine enough for my dad to lay into me for a good five minutes about coming back to Boston. When my father's health returned, so, it seemed, did his crusade to get me to move. When I told him I was coming this spring—Dawn would be gone and I'd have nothing left tethering me to Allen- hurst—he accused me of crying wolf. I was damned if I did, damned if I didn't. The resulting foul mood caused me to beg off a poker game I was supposed to go to with some friends, friends who had threatened to come to my house and drag me bodily to the game.

I hadn't thought they would really do it. Damn it, I

didn't feel like human interaction right now. I didn't want to see anyone.

I swung the door open and barked, "What?"

Correction: I didn't want to see anyone except her.

She looked different, more like her old self. It was partly because she'd done her hair and makeup, but partly because she was smiling, apparently of her own volition. I'd seen a few smiles in recent months, but I'd had to coax each and every one out of her.

Her eyes slid down from where they'd been on my face. Shit. I wasn't wearing a shirt. I'd taken it off during a bout of anger-fueled weight lifting earlier. Well, hell, it wasn't illegal to be shirtless in your own house.

Her smile grew larger, and I felt the tips of my ears heat.

"There's going to be a total lunar eclipse tonight," she said.

"I know." I was relieved I hadn't been scheduled to work. Rare celestial occurrences that happened at night did not mix well with college kids.

"I was wondering if, um…" She grew shy then, her gaze dropping to the floor as she shifted from one foot to the other. "You seem to know a lot about nature and stuff around here, and I…was wondering if you knew of anywhere good to watch it." She looked back up at me.

The mere sight of her, standing in the dim light of my porch, putting herself out there, had my anger dissipating. I grinned—I couldn't help it. "I do indeed."

Her answering smile was like a shot of adrenaline.

"Give me thirty seconds to throw on a shirt."

Twenty minutes later, we were climbing the twisty stone stairway that led to Salter Tower. The two-hundred-year-old clock tower rose from the oldest building on campus and was locked up tight. After a rash of incidents in the 1960s, including one in which an acid-tripping kid had nearly jumped and had to be rescued by the fire department, the college got serious about security. Clock maintenance and repair were the only reasons anyone was allowed up there these days. At all other times, the massive wooden doors at the base were securely locked and armed with an alarm.

But I had the keys, and I knew the code.

"Officer Perez, I didn't take you for such a rule-breaker," Dawn said as I punched in another code at a second, alarmed door at the top of the stairs. She was panting from the steep ascent, and it did something to me.

"It's Art," I said. "I'm not on duty."

"Art," she repeated, still breathless, and it did something more to me. Damn it, I was trying to *help* Dawn. If I couldn't prevent myself from thinking inappropriate thoughts about her at home, I could at least refrain from doing so in her presence.

The tower was open to the night on all four sides, and she made her way to the western side of the enclosure, where the moon was most visible. "This is amazing!" she exclaimed. "I never even realized that people could come up here!"

I joined her and set up a camping lantern I'd brought, gratified that I had made her so happy. There were overhead lights in the tower enclosure, but using them would mean risking detection. I would douse the camping light when the eclipse started in earnest, but for now, I set it to its dimmest level as we got settled. I unpacked the bag of goodies we'd bought at an all-night convenience store on our way—a box of Smurfberry Crunch and a can of Tab for her, and a bag of corn nuts and a bottle of water for me.

"The people look like little dolls," she said, leaning over the deep stone ledge that ringed the space.

"Whoa." I put my hand on her back. She was perfectly safe, but I'd reacted instinctively to seeing her leaning out over the edge like that.

"I love that we're up here, and they have no idea." She leaned back into my hand and smiling up at me. She pulled off her mittens, grabbed her cereal box, and tore it open. "Yum!" she said, grabbing a handful of the unnaturally red and blue "berries." Seeing her munching on the cartoon cereal, I was reminded of how young she was.

It should have made me uncomfortable. But for once, I didn't care. Maybe it was the strange out-of-time-ness of it, of being perched physically above campus like gods on our own collegiate Mount Olympus while we waited for the moon to transit into Earth's shadow. Whatever the reason, the air felt electric, alive despite the cold, snowy December night.

"I've never seen an eclipse before," she said as the first sliver of moon moved into the shadows.

"I always think it's going to be more dramatic than it is," I said. "The moon never totally disappears. It just gets very dim—like you would miss it if you didn't know to look for it."

"But you know," she said. "You know to look for it."

We had been standing a few feet apart, both of us leaning our forearms on the ledge, and I glanced over at her, trying to make sense of what she was saying.

She slid over until she was right next to me, her

forearm touching mine. Her shoulder stopped midway up my upper arm, which meant her head was exactly the right height for resting on my shoulder.

Which she did.

I did not pull away.

We watched the whole eclipse like that, or at least the part where the moon was totally obscured by the sun. It glowed a very faint red, and we stood there in silence watching it for nearly an hour. It reminded me of those pictures you see of Jesus or of the Virgin Mother (all those years of Catholic school were still in there somewhere) where you can see their hearts showing through their clothing. Except instead of glowing brightly, this heart, this moon-heart, grew dimmer and dimmer, until it was almost not there.

"Do you remember when you came to my apartment, and I said my heart was missing?" Dawn said, her voice coming out all shaky.

Oh, Jesus, that was exactly it. *This* was exactly *that*. I put my arm around her, so that instead of standing next to me with her head resting on my shoulder, she was tucked into the crook of my arm. I held her tight.

She didn't say anything more, nor did I. We didn't need to.

DAWN

When we got back Art's car, it was after two in the morning. "Let's get you home," he said as he started the car, and I almost jumped. We had been enrobed in silence for so long, and not just any silence—a deep, extreme silence, in which I'd felt myself come through something. As stupid as it sounded, I almost felt like I'd witnessed myself being reborn gradually into the night the same way the moon had emerged from the shadows.

"Or we could go to your place," I said firmly, sending my own strong voice out to pierce the silence, too, to name what I wanted. He whipped his gaze to mine, but it was too dark to see what was in his eyes. Then he let his head fall back like he was appealing to heaven for help and emitted a strangled sort of half-moan.

I lost some of my nerve then, was beginning to fear I had made myself ridiculous—*again*. Why had I thought I deserved this? That just because I wanted something, I could have it? Hadn't I left that part of myself behind?

Hadn't Julianne taken it with her?

He sat up and shifted the car into "drive." We pulled away from the tower so quickly that his tires squealed a little.

And we didn't turn onto the road we needed to go down to get to my building.

No. We went the opposite way—toward his house.

My skin started to prickle like I had come into a warm house from a very cold night.

He didn't speak as he drove, merely stared at the road, his mouth a grim line of determination. He took the corners so fast, it was like being in one of those Atari racing games. But he remained in absolute control. I felt almost like we were in the police cruiser, the way we were hurtling down the deserted streets of campus. I was exhilarated and scared and turned on all at once—all feelings I had thought I was too permanently broken to ever experience again.

When we reached his house, I paused for a moment in the passenger seat. I wasn't afraid, not exactly, but I knew that if we were going to do what I thought we were going to do—what I *hoped* we were going to do—it was going to be totally different than my past experiences. Heck, you could tell from the way he drove.

He'd come around to open my door while I was pausing to gather my courage. He gave me his hand, and I took it, letting him help me up from the low-to-the-ground sports car. He pulled, and as I came to my feet, he kept pulling, stopping only when I was mashed against his chest, my breasts compressing almost painfully against the solid wall of him as he wrapped his arms around me.

I thought he was going to kiss me—was in the middle of tilting my head back to facilitate a kiss, in fact—but he did not.

"Are you sure about this, Dawn?"

I nodded.

"That's not good enough. Are you sure about this, Dawn?" he said, repeating his question in a gruff, almost angry tone.

"Yes." I tried to summon that confident, self-assured voice I'd found when I asked him to take me home. "I want this."

"Why?" His eyes searched my face like it was a treasure map. "Why do you want this?"

"Because you make me feel good," I whispered. "Because I haven't felt good for so long." *Maybe ever*, I added silently.

He released me then and grabbed my hand and led me up the driveway. Once through the front door, he unzipped my coat and pushed it off my shoulders, letting it fall to the floor, then he did the same with his own.

"What do you want, Dawn?"

"I told you, I want to feel good."

He shook his head. "It's not enough." When I started to protest, he held up a hand and said, "Remember blah, blah, blah?"

I nodded, miserable because it seemed like he was going to put the brakes on.

"Well, it's not just blah, blah, blah. I'm older than you by a not-insignificant number of years. I work at Allenhurst. You're a student."

"For another week, technically. But classes are done. It's only finals left. And there's not anything specifically prohibiting…" I trailed off, realizing that to say any more would only make me look desperate. I had scoured the college's policies before I interviewed Julianne, looking for anything governing staff-student relationships, so I knew that technically, we weren't breaking that rule at least.

"You're vulnerable right now," he said, delivering the stake to my new moon of a heart, because he and I both knew it was true. But then, when I hung my head, preemptively waiting for the shame to wash over me, I saw his erection. It was impossible to miss. Instead of his usual jeans, he'd been wearing gray sweatpants when I knocked on his door earlier, and now they were tented. Very tented.

"So look me in the eyes, Dawn, and tell me exactly what it is you want."

That erection gave me hope. It made me brave. So I looked up. I even reached over and switched on the light in his entryway so there would be no mistaking my intentions. My heart was pounding like it wanted to flee my chest, but I managed to make the words come out clear and calm.

"I want to have sex with you."

"All right then." In one fluid motion, he grabbed the back of his T-shirt and pulled it off. And, oh, Richard

Gere in *American Gigolo* had nothing on this guy. Rob Lowe, Scott Baio, name your *Tiger Beat* hunk. He left them all in the dust.

He came at me then, picking me up so I was at his level, and nuzzling my throat. "This is how this is going to work," he said, using his teeth to gently scrape down to my collarbone, where he started pressing urgent, open-mouthed kisses. "I require not just consent, but continuous consent."

I moaned.

"Not good enough," he said sharply, pulling away and setting me back on my feet.

So, since there was no way I was walking away from this, I grabbed his hand and headed toward his hallway. We paused at the first door, and I peeked in, but it appeared to be a home gym, littered as it was with weights and benches.

"I'm looking for the bedroom," I said, emboldened not only by his still-tented sweatpants, but by the fact that I was shaking with need.

"Next door." He nodded down the hall and let me lead him there.

When we arrived, I went to the windows and lowered the blinds. He turned on a small lamp on a nightstand. "What now?" he said.

I went to him, lifted myself up on my tiptoes, and grabbed his head, intending to pull him down for a kiss, but he resisted.

"I need to hear you say it," he said.

"I want you to kiss me," I said, "And I want to kiss you."

It was his turn to moan as he lowered his head. It was as if once he'd heard me explicitly request a kiss, it lit a fire in him. His lips crashed down on mine, and his whole body shuddered as I opened my mouth to receive his tongue. We clung to each other, kissing deeply, aggressively licking into each other's mouths. I let my hands trail up and down his muscled back. I wanted him to touch me too, so I broke for a moment to pull my own shirt over my head. I had just been wearing a camisole under my shirt—my breasts were small enough that I didn't really need a bra—and I caught it along with my shirt, which left me standing before him totally exposed as my aching nipples tightened even more under his gaze.

I was desperate for him to touch me, to take away some of the ache—which was what he was always doing, really, when I thought about it. So I grabbed his hands and brought them to my breasts.

He hissed, almost like I was hurting him, and ground out, "Say it."

"I want you to touch my breasts," I said quickly. "I want you to put your mouth on them, too."

And, just like that, he did. He kneaded them both, one in each hand, as he lowered his mouth to one nipple and sucked. Lust lanced through me, a sharp spike connecting that nipple with my vagina. In soothing one ache, he'd transferred the almost painful need somewhere else, and I writhed against him.

He must have known—of course he knew; Art always knew—because he moved a hand to the waistband of my jeans. I followed him, fumbling to undo the button fly, but when I had my pants shoved down over my hips, his hand remained where it was, hovering. "I want you to touch me," I said, getting the hang of this continuous consent thing. Hell, I was getting off on it. Being able to tell him exactly what I wanted and have him comply was a huge turn-on. And he wasn't just complying. With each additional increment of our intimacy, as soon as I vocalized what I wanted, he pounced, like a hunter who'd been holding back his lethal strength.

He dipped a finger into my wet folds, and as I gasped, I walked backward toward his bed, pulling him along with me. When the backs of my legs hit the mattress, I let myself fall, taking him with me. "I want to take off my pants," I said, keeping up the stream of talk for fear he would put the brakes on otherwise. "I want you to take off your pants, too. I want to be naked with you."

I shimmied the rest of the way out of my jeans as I spoke, and he practically growled as he whipped off his sweatpants and underwear, watching me all the while. No one had ever looked at me like that. Like I was enough. No—like I was *everything*.

He fell to his knees, which startled me, and I started to sit up.

"I want to taste you," he said gruffly. "I want to put my mouth on your pussy and taste you." His eyes never left mine as he made those shocking declarations. "Is that okay?"

"Yes," I said, even though, in truth, the idea made me a little nervous. I had never done that. It wasn't something that had been in the repertoire of the boys I'd been with. But hadn't I been thinking, back that first time we kissed, that Arturo was a *man*? I knew he would stop the moment I asked him to. And I trusted him to make me feel good.

"Ohhh!" I breathed as his mouth made contact with my tender, engorged flesh. It was a different sensation than when I masturbated, which had been, heretofore, my only reliable method of getting off. It was less focused but somehow more intense for it. He wasn't even applying much pressure, just licking my opening like he would an ice cream cone, teasing my clit gently at the top of every lick. And he was making noises of appreciation almost like he *was* eating an ice cream cone.

"You taste so good," he whispered, breaking his rhythm enough to look up at me. "Are you okay?"

I nodded frantically. "I want to come with you inside me," I nearly shouted, shocking the hell out of myself. But I was close, and I didn't want this to end without feeling my body stretching to accommodate him. "Please."

He grinned. "Well, let's see what we can do about that then, shall we?" He popped up and moved to the nightstand and began rummaging around in its top drawer. I took a moment to catch my breath and admire him from afar. His bottom half was as gorgeous and muscular as his top.

When he turned, he was rolling a condom onto a very large erection. *Definitely not a boy,* I thought, and I laughed from the sheer joy of it, even as I said, "You don't need that. I'm on the pill."

"That may be," he said. "But you should always use condoms regardless, Dawn." I wanted to say that I was never going to have sex with anyone besides him again, that he had ruined me for other people, but of course you didn't just *say* stuff like that. And I had no idea if he was regarding this as a onetime thing. Heck, I had no idea if *I* was regarding this as onetime thing.

He moved toward me, but instead of climbing on top of me, he surprised me by lying next to me on the bed, on his back, his ridiculously impressive erection pointing at the ceiling. He grabbed my arm and pulled me toward him, just enough that he could reach my face. He smiled and stroked my cheek. "I want you to come with me inside you, too. I want to feel you clenching, squeezing my cock until my head nearly explodes." The plain, almost-clinical statement of desire ratcheted my own lust up about a thousand percent as he moved his hand to take mine, holding it like he was helping me into a carriage in an old-fashioned movie.

I realized he was waiting for *me* to climb on top of *him*.

So I did, shivering as a mixture of lust and anticipation and nervousness moved through me.

I kept hold of his one hand and pressed against his chest with my other to brace myself, watching his face as I sank down onto him.

"Shiiiiittt," he groaned, using the hand that wasn't holding mine to punch the mattress next to him. His reaction was both startling and gratifying.

It had been a while since I'd done this. It had been *years* since I'd done this, actually. I stayed still for a moment to let myself adjust to the unfamiliar stretching sensation, and to the knowledge that I had allowed someone else inside my body.

"Are you okay?" he asked, his eyes glittering.

"Stop asking me that," I whispered as I began lifting myself off him. "I am very, very okay."

He smiled, but his grin disappeared quickly as I sank back down onto his length, impaling myself a little more deeply than I had before.

"Shit!" he said again, but the word wasn't drawn out this time; it was short and clipped and almost angry. His eyes closed.

"You're going to have to think of something else to say," I teased, but I secretly loved the fact that I had reduced this powerful, utterly competent man to a single word.

His eyes flew open, and I laughed to show him I was teasing, but also because I couldn't believe how...right this felt.

"How about this then?" he rasped. "Shit, you feel amazing. So tight and wet that I never want this to be over, but at the same time, so tight and wet that I'm afraid this will be over too soon." And with that, he reached up and pressed a thumb against my clit.

I was already turned on, but that little touch shoved me way farther down the road. I didn't want to talk anymore, *couldn't* talk anymore. I rode him as he kneaded my clit, bracing myself now with both hands on his chest, meeting his unbroken gaze. It was intense, having that kind of eye contact. It made me realize how much I hadn't done that before, how my sexual experiences had been about closing my eyes and sort of...imagining something else. He wouldn't let me, though. Well, that wasn't actually true, of course. Mr. Continuous Consent was going to be down with whatever I wanted, I knew, but it was like his eyes had so much power over me that I simply couldn't look away, couldn't sever that connection.

"Oh!" I shouted, as he pushed me even closer to the edge. "I'm going to come!" I had never been a screamer before. Maybe because it always seemed improper somehow, or maybe because when I was having sex before, it was usually furtive, needed to be hidden from parents or roommates. But to be able to make whatever noises I wanted to, as loud as I wanted to. Well, it was hot. It was like a continuation of his continuous consent thing. In being so careful to make sure I knew that nothing was going to happen unless I wanted it to, in making me name my desires, he somehow also paved the way for me to do and say exactly what I needed to realize those desires.

I came like a jackhammer, shrieking the whole time.

He grabbed my hips and took control of the rhythm, pistoning into me like a man on fire.

"Yes!" I shouted, because I didn't want him to stop himself, to realize he'd forgotten to make me specifically say I wanted him to do that. I didn't want him to lose momentum.

He flipped me, picking me up and rolling on top of me, continuing to pound into me, but somehow managing to keep his hand on my clit. "Keep going!" I encouraged. I wanted him to come. I wanted him to feel as amazing as I did.

But then, oh, but then...my exhortations became more urgent. My legs wrapped around his waist, almost of their own volition, to try to alter the angle slightly so I could—

"I'm going to come again," I panted, astonished. That had never happened to me before. I'd read about it in *Cosmo*, but, oh my God, I hadn't known.

He cried out, slumping against me but keeping his magical fingers moving. It only took a few more seconds for me to join him in falling over the edge.

I lay there shaking, aftershocks rippling through me as he pulled out and dealt with the condom.

Then he came back to bed and lay on his side next to me, head propped on one hand.

"Shit," I said.

He smiled and nodded. "Shit."

CHAPTER TEN

ARTURO

When I woke up the next morning with Dawn in my arms and a raging boner, I waited for the regrets to come seeping in.

They did not.

As she sighed and shifted, drawing my attention to her beautiful, makeup-smeared face, I couldn't find one single thing to be sorry about. Probably we should have waited a few weeks until she graduated, but, honestly, I couldn't find it in me to care at that moment.

I had never had sex like that before. I sounded like I was in a fucking romance novel, but there had been something beyond just sex going on last night. Beyond making love, even. I'd had girlfriends I'd loved—or thought I had—and this...wasn't that. Watching her ride me, looking deeply into her eyes as she surrendered to me even as she took possession of my soul, had been beyond my imaginings.

She owned me. This slip of a girl *owned* me.

And I was completely fine with that. So fine that I actually laughed out loud.

It must have woken her, because she pressed against the enclosure of my arms. I released her and watched her stretch like a cat, all that gorgeous porcelain skin laid out before me. I wanted to touch it all at once, put my hands all over it, mark it as mine. I wanted her to tell me it was okay to do all that.

She looked like a cat, too, when she opened her eyes, a small, sly smile spreading across her face. "Good morning," she said, the feline smile growing wider.

"I want to taste you again," I said, seized with the need. She'd interrupted me last night as I'd been feasting on her. Not that I was complaining, but I needed more. More of her. "I've felt you coming on my cock, but now I want to feel you coming on my mouth."

She giggled, which I took for assent, but I paused anyway.

"Enough with this continuous consent thing," she teased.

"Eventually, we will move from continuous consent to singular consent."

"Eventually," she echoed, and part of me wondered if I'd been too presumptive. I'd been so over-the-top with the consent thing because I was so wary of the age and power differentials between us and of the emotional wringer she'd been through this past fall. So many people in Dawn's life had let her down, had "not seen her." I wasn't *ever* going to be one of those people.

But I also wasn't letting her go. There was going to be an eventually.

So I said, firmly, "Yes, eventually."

She paused, and I prayed I hadn't spooked her. But I

didn't want to pretend that this had been a one-night stand. Dawn and I had struck some kind of beautiful, unspoken deal where we called things what they were. We had always done that, in fact, had always spoken honestly with each other, even when we were at odds over some petty crime or other.

She pressed her lips together, and for a moment, I thought she was going to cry. That she was going to get up and take her heart, which had come through its own eclipse, out of my bedroom and out of my life. What she didn't know was that if she did that, she'd be taking mine, too.

But then her face lightened. "So continuous consent eventually gives way to singular consent. That means, like, once per encounter, right?" She was teasing me, trying not to smile.

"Yes," I said. "But of course it can be revoked at any time."

She nodded and touched me, starting at my abs and letting her hands slide up my chest. "And what about implied consent? When do we get to that?"

"What do you mean by implied consent?" I choked out, trying to pay attention to her and not to the wave of lust she was summoning inside me with the lightest of touches.

"Well…" She trailed off, tracing a finger lazily around one of my nipples. "Let's say we were lying around one morning and you happened to notice"—she grabbed my hand and pulled it beneath the sheets, shoving it between her legs, where it found a glorious slick of moisture—"that I was dripping wet because I wanted you so badly. But maybe I didn't outright say anything. I didn't say, 'Arturo, please go down on me.' What would happen then?"

Jesus, she was so impossibly hot. I could hardly stand it. But I was serious about my stance, even if I was over-doing it. "I wouldn't do anything," I said. "But let the record show that it would kill me."

She shoved the sheets down, kicking her legs free of them and letting them fall open. "In that case, Arturo, please go down on me."

So I did.

And then I got up and made her breakfast, and when she grabbed the pancake batter from me and poured it into the shape of a heart on my griddle I thought, *I love you.* I almost said it too, carried away by the intoxicating feeling of the naked honesty that had characterized our recent time together.

But the phone rang. I was prepared to ignore it, but when I didn't move after the first couple of rings, she swatted me away and said, "Get your phone. I got these pancakes."

It was Manny.

"What's wrong?" I said, because I just knew. Dawn looked up, concern etched into her otherwise-smooth features.

"Dad had another heart attack."

"And?" I pressed.

"It's bad this time. They're doing a triple bypass this afternoon."

"Christ." I walked as far as the phone cord would let me, wanting to look out the window for some reason but falling short. "Is he conscious?"

"He was. They have him heavily sedated now because he was so agitated."

"I'll be there as soon as I can," I said calmly, like the world wasn't crumbling around me.

I didn't even bother putting the phone back in its cradle, just let it clatter to the floor as I covered the final few steps to the kitchen window, which overlooked my snow-covered back yard. I pressed my forehead against the cold glass. This shouldn't have been a surprise. And yet…

"What's wrong?" Her small arms snaked around me from behind, and she pressed herself against my back. I was generally an isolationist when it came to grief, usually didn't want people in my face and in my space when shit was going down. But for some reason, with her, I didn't mind.

So I turned and said, "My dad had another heart attack. I've got to go home."

"Of course," she said, her eyes widening.

I shook my head. She wasn't understanding. "No. I think I finally have to…really go home.

She took my hand, led me to one of the kitchen chairs, pushed me back onto it, and climbed into my lap.

"Go back now, yes, of course. Stay as long as you need to. But you don't have to move back to Boston if you don't want to, Art." Then she kissed my cheek and added, "It's okay to want what you want. Don't let other people live your life for you—you're smarter than that."

My breath caught as I recognized the words. They were the ones I had said to her when she told me she was considering a master's in journalism at the expense of doing something with her psychology degree.

Then it hitched again as I realized the truth in them.

And just in case I hadn't, she smiled and brushed away a tear I hadn't realized was making its way down my cheek and added, "If it's true for me, then it's true for you, too."

DAWN

By the time Art pulled up at my apartment half an hour after his brother called, I was totally confused. Not that he was doing anything to confuse me, more that I was doubting my own sense of what was happening between us. I'd woken that morning with the residue of the previous night's self-confidence still with me. We'd had a fun, sexy morning in which I hadn't once thought about my problems. I wasn't kidding myself that Art magically had the power to make my troubles disappear, but when I was with him, whether we were having sex or making pancakes, I was fully there. It was that same sense of relief, of respite, that walking and talking with him had given me earlier in the semester, but more.

But now he was going to Boston. For how long, I wasn't sure. I wasn't sure he was, either, but he'd hastily packed a suitcase and was going to leave directly after dropping me off. He'd let me comfort him, hold him, after he got the phone call, but he hadn't said much.

Anyway, it didn't really matter how long he was going to be gone, did it? Because it wasn't like we were going to ride off into the sunset and get married. He'd told me that night at Delta Chi that I'd rescued myself from Royce. I needed to do the same now—take my exams and figure out what was next, without pinning any responsibility on him.

I was struggling to figure out what to say as we pulled up to my building. "I hope…" Crap, I didn't know what I hoped. "I hope your father is okay," I finished lamely, because that much at least was true. The rest was all a jumble of conflicting emotions in my heart. *I hope you come back soon. I hope last night meant as much to you as it did to me. I hope I won't need you forever to feel good. I hope I can make something of my life. I hope...* "Oh my God."

"What?" He spoke sharply, looking around as he pulled over in front of my building, like he was assessing the place for the presence of bad guys. "What's wrong?"

I couldn't believe it. In my three and a half years here, he'd never once shown up on campus. Not for homecoming, not for parents' weekend. I don't even think he had called. I'd called him a few times—though usually when I needed something, I spoke to his assistant—but that was the extent of it.

But there he was, standing next to his black town car, as out of place as you'd expect him to be in this neighborhood of slightly ramshackle student housing.

"Dawn," Art said, his tone infused with urgency. "What is it?"

I shook my head as if maybe that would clear my vision, sweep away the mirage before me. But no, he was still there, and he'd caught sight of me and was walking toward Art's car.

"It's my father," I said.

Daddy looked as out of place at my small kitchen table as he had outside my building. But maybe it wasn't my apartment so much as it was...my life. My father was out of place in my life. It was the first time I'd thought of it in those terms, and it made me sad.

"Are you going to show me what that is?" I asked, as I handed him a cup of tea I knew he wouldn't drink. Making it had given me something to do with my nervous energy.

He had been clutching an envelope when we pulled up in Art's car. He'd passed it from hand to hand like it was something fragile when he'd shaken hands with Art after my awkward introduction. I hadn't known what to call Art. I wasn't presuming "boyfriend," but "friend" seemed off base too. In the end, I hadn't called him anything, had just used his name. And he'd been so preoccupied with his own father's problems that I'm not even sure he noticed my lack of finesse.

The envelope was now lying facedown on my kitchen table. It had been slit at the top with a letter opener. Daddy slid it over to me, and I flipped it. It was addressed to me. I wanted to take him to task for invading my privacy, but there was no point. I had long ago learned that my father did what he liked, and to suggest that he do otherwise was a waste of energy.

The return address was that of Columbia University, which made no sense. I had no reason to be corresponding with Columbia. Warily, I slid a letter out of the envelope and scanned it.

"It's an acceptance letter from the journalism school," my father said, with what sounded like excitement in his tone, but I wasn't sure, because Daddy didn't really do excitement.

"I can see that," I began slowly. "But I didn't apply to Columbia." I hadn't applied anywhere. It was too late for the spring semester, and my mind was in such a muddle that I'd thought I'd get through finals and then worry about a game plan for the rest of the year and beyond— whether that included grad school or something else. And even if I had gotten my act together for spring semester grad school, I would never have applied to Columbia. I was expecting great grades this semester because I'd thrown myself into studying as a distraction, but they wouldn't be enough to make up for my previous lackluster performance.

My father quirked a smile. "You actually did."

I let the letter flutter to the table. My father was one of those powerful men who did what he wanted, took what he wanted. I had a flashback to the events of last night, of Art, another powerful man. But Art didn't take things. He asked. He made you *want* to give them.

"You can start in January."

"But that's…impossible." I didn't know why I was protesting. Nothing was impossible when you were Edward Hathaway, media titan. Especially when what you were trying to do was get your kid into journalism school.

"I showed the dean your story," he said. "Both of them, actually—the one about the football player, too."

I shook my head. Part of me wanted to ask what Daddy had promised. Money? Access to jobs and internships at his outlets? Because even if the dean had been impressed, the J-school at Columbia didn't let in gossips with 3.0 GPAs and no legitimate journalism experience to speak of. Even Jenny, the academic and editing superstar, said she wouldn't get in without some real-world experience under her belt.

"The dean was as impressed as I was."

I couldn't have been more shocked if he had slapped me across the face.

"You were…impressed?" I hated the way my voice sounded, all small and needy. But I couldn't help it. I had gone through a straight-A phase in early high school—after my acting-out phase of late junior high—and I'd never gotten an "impressed."

"Those pieces were serious investigative journalism."

JENNY HOLIDAY

A lovely warm feeling started spreading through my chest at the praise.

"You did them a disservice by calling them gossip."

"Well, my column had a sort of existing brand, see—"

He waved a hand dismissively as he got up and paced my small living room while I remained at the table in the adjacent kitchen, stunned. "Once you shed that gossip veneer, get rid of the fluffy, emotion-driven stuff—"

It was my turn to interrupt him. "But emotions were the whole point in those two stories." *I was trying to get justice for people who were suffering,* I wanted to add, but I feared that to do so would make me sound humiliatingly naïve.

He wasn't listening, anyway. "The thrill of getting the story. Of seeing your game-changing words in print." He paced back to the table and smiled at me, which had the counterintuitive effect of making me want to cry. "I have to say, I never knew you had it in you, Dawn."

It *wasn't* about the thrill of the story for me, though. I'd begun the column for entirely selfish reasons, banking on it to make me popular. If I had come to take any kind of deeper satisfaction from it, it was *because* of its emotional nature. Because people were so fascinating—in the way they behaved in relation to their values, their secret yearnings, their fears.

"It's a two-year program, so by January of '86, you'll be able to write your ticket. I'll put you on any paper you want. Or maybe broadcast. With some work on your hair and makeup, you could be pretty enough for TV."

Maybe journalism wouldn't be so bad. I hadn't hated some of the arts and entertainment profiles Jenny had talked me into doing over the years. I'd even gotten to interview a famous artist who was an alum—he'd been a

120

virtual recluse and hadn't granted any media interviews for years before he talked to me.

"And nobody will ever expect such a small girl to be a hard-hitting journalist. You'll always have the element of surprise working for you."

He pulled out a chair and sat back down at the table. "And maybe you'll keep following in my footsteps. Do a decade or so in the trenches, and then you can assume an executive position at Hathaway Media." He patted my head. "But I'm getting ahead of myself, aren't I?" He slid a paper toward me, one that had been in the same envelope as the acceptance letter. "I just need you to sign here, and I'll take care of the rest. You can pick up right where you left off with that story about that girl. Figure out what the next story is."

And maybe get it right next time, said my inner critic.

He rolled his pen across the table, and it sounded like thunder in my ears. What was the matter with me? I was usually pretty fearless. I'd stolen Ace three—almost four—times. I'd talked my way onto the college newspaper, creating a niche out of nothing. So why was my heart beating so hard it felt like it was going to pop out of my chest?

"I'm so proud of you, Dawn," said my father. "You've got, what? Another week here for finals? Then you can come home."

I signed.

CHAPTER ELEVEN

December 20, 1983

Dear Art,

I probably should have just left a message on your answering machine, but this felt like something that shouldn't be done over the phone.

I hope your father is okay. (Is it too macabre to say that I have been reading the Boston obituaries and have been relieved not to see his name?) I'm including the phone number of my father's apartment, and I hope you'll call and let me know how he's doing.

I came back to New York after I finished my exams because I've decided to start grad school in journalism at Columbia this spring semester. It was kind of sudden—classes start January 7—but I think it will be good.

I wanted to thank you for everything you've done for me (well, except maybe for that first ticket). You really looked out for me over the years. And when I was reeling after Julianne's death, you kept me sane. And everything else... well, thank you. You're a good cop, and an even better man.

Sincerely,
Dawn

ARTURO

Sincerely? What the fuck?

I didn't usually have much of a temper. I wasn't Fuller, busting into parties gunning for conflict. But when, a week after I'd dropped Dawn off at her apartment and hightailed it to my father's bedside, I returned to my house to find her letter in my mailbox, I punched through the drywall in my foyer. My family had thought I was insane to be running back to campus when I was planning to be in Boston for the holidays anyway. What was so important in Allenhurst that it couldn't wait until the new year?

A Dear John letter, apparently.

"God*damn* it!" I deserved the burst of pain that exploded through my hand. I'd been cursing myself the past several days for not having had the wherewithal to get Dawn's phone number before I'd left. She had mine all these years, since I'd given her that business card, but I didn't have hers, preferring instead to intercept her in person when I needed to see her.

So the moment the doctors pronounced that Dad was

going to be okay, I'd come rushing back to Allenhurst. I felt awful about how abruptly we'd ended our time together the other morning, and I didn't want to leave things a moment longer than necessary without telling her...everything. There was so much to say.

And now she was in fucking journalism school? I wanted to punch the wall with my other hand, but I was smart enough to realize that I would need it to dial the phone number she'd left me.

"Hathaway residence," said a woman's voice, its formality suggesting it belonged to a housekeeper or servant of some sort.

I cleared my throat. "May I speak to Dawn please?"

"May I ask who's calling, please?"

"Arturo Perez."

"Just a moment, sir, I'll see if Miss Hathaway is available."

Miss Hathaway. My heart clenched to hear her name the way I used to say it. I started shaking as I listened to the rustling sound of a phone being put down. I took a deep breath. It would be okay. We would sort things out.

"Hello? Art? How is your dad?"

"What are you doing in New York, Dawn?" Shit. That had come out wrong. I was confused, but I wasn't angry. At least not at her.

There was a long pause. I'd hurt her by speaking so sharply, so I sighed and said, "My dad is out of surgery. The extent of his recovery remains to be seen."

"I thought you'd still be in Boston, but it sounds like you...got my letter."

"I did, and I call bullshit. You don't want to do journalism."

"It's not that I don't want to so much as—"

"What happened to 'it's okay to want what you want'? What happened to 'don't let other people live your life for you'?" I still hadn't managed to temper my angry tone, but I was beginning not to care. I needed to jolt her back to her senses. "You told me those things. And you know what? I told them to my family. When my father woke up, he started right in on me, and I just looked at him and told him I wasn't leaving Allenhurst."

"I'm so glad. I—"

"And you know why I did that, Dawn?" I was rudely interrupting, but I didn't care. I had to finish. "Why, after years of hemming and hawing because I didn't want to disappoint him, did I man the fuck up and tell him the truth? Because of you, Dawn. Because your bravery this past semester has been a goddamned inspiration." I almost chickened out about saying the rest, but I figured a guy couldn't make a speech on the merits of bravery and then not go all the way. "And because I wanted to be the sort of man who was worthy of you."

There was a long silence, then her voice, a shaky, tentative whisper. "I'm not as brave as you think I am."

"If you want to go to grad school, great. If you want to go to Columbia, great." It wasn't, but that wasn't the point. "But psychology, not journalism. Learn from me. Don't invest years trying to please your father."

"You think the situations are the same," Dawn said, her voice gathering strength, even beginning to sound a bit annoyed. "You think we have these mirror-image disapproving fathers. But they're *not* the same. Underneath everything, your father has always loved you."

I was tempted to insist that the same was true about her father, but I actually didn't think it was. I had never lied to Dawn, and I wasn't going to start now.

"Anyway," she went on, "it's not about my father—or at least not only about him."

"What is it about then?"

"Julianne."

"Excuse me?"

"I've been thinking… I know this sounds lame. But I've been thinking that if I could do it over again—"

"You can't. She's dead." It was harsh, but she needed to be reminded.

"I know. But if I could learn the proper way of doing things, maybe next time I could write a story that would serve justice but also…not hurt people."

"Or you could be a psychologist. Or a counselor. Or a social worker. Or a *cop*. There are so many ways to help people, Dawn, if that's your aim."

"I know, but—"

I could feel her slipping away from me. "I'm going to apply for a promotion in the department here," I said quickly. "Sergeant. The captain wants me to take a couple classes first, but he says he'll consider me in the spring. So I'm actually going to be an Allenhurst student myself this coming semester. I'm taking a night class. Youth Crime and Justice." I wanted her to really see that I'd meant what I'd said to my family: my life was in Allenhurst. "It's part of the master's in criminology program. If I like it, I might do the degree."

"Julianne was going to switch to criminology," Dawn whispered.

"What?" That had caught me off guard.

"She told me that in our interview. She'd flunked out of sociology, and of course she wasn't keen on going on in communication after what happened. So she was going to do criminology. Third time's a charm, she'd said. I told her it was a great idea, that maybe she could go on to law school and put away people like Daniels. She told me she appreciated the sentiment, but that she wasn't smart enough for law school."

"Dawn. You can't..." I didn't know what to say. Well, I did, but I was afraid maybe I'd exhausted my supply of bravery.

"I have to go," she said.

"I love you," I said.

But she had already hung up. I was speaking to a dial tone.

DAWN

I knew when I set foot inside the apartment that the party had been a mistake. But as I was swarmed at the door by a trio of girls I'd gone to high school with, I allowed myself to be swept inside as they lobbed New Year's greetings at me.

"Oh my God, Dawn. I can't believe what happened!" said one.

"How are you handling things?" said another with what was clearly false concern. I couldn't even remember her name. We'd been only nodding acquaintances at school.

I decided to shock them with an honest answer. "Actually, not very well."

But it made no impact. It was like they didn't even hear it. They just kept chattering as one of them took my coat and the other handed me a beer and ushered me farther into the apartment.

The swanky penthouse was full of the twentysome-thing versions of my old friends. I hadn't seen most of them since high school. They were slightly older, but elementally the same. Everyone was well-dressed in the latest fashions, and they all looked slightly bored in the way that only rich kids can.

Something changed in the air when they noticed me. Conversations stopped, leaving the room silent except for the Eurythmics coming from a set of speakers in the corner.

I made eye contact with a guy sitting on the corner of a sofa. He lifted a beer to me in a toast. It was Nate, one of my old high school boyfriends. With his feathered blond hair and his rugby shirt with upturned collar, he looked so...young. I gave him a wave.

"Well, shit," he said, breaking the silence, "If I'd known you were going to become famous, Dawn, I never would have broken up with you."

He meant it as a joke, so I smiled wanly, and others laughed. The girl next to him raised her beer too, and said, "To Dawn, our famous friend. We always knew you had it in you."

But you didn't, I wanted to say. *None of us have spoken, not really, for four years.*

Soon the whole party was toasting me and clapping. I spent the next few minutes...well, receiving people. People lined up to talk to me like they were wedding guests and I was the bride. At first, I tried to make small talk, but I had trouble shaking people, and each conversation seemed longer than the last, no matter what I said. I even started being borderline rude, but it made no difference. It was like they were made of Teflon.

Then the invitations started coming. My old friend Claire wanted to know if I wanted to go shopping tomorrow. A couple girls invited me to spend spring break with them in Florida. There was a New Year's Day brunch tomorrow at someone else's parents' place, a cocktail party next week.

The realization hit me with a thud. Everyone wanted me. I was popular. This was what I had spent all of high school—and college—working for.

And I was as lonely as ever. Lonelier.

"I have to go."

"You just got here," Nate protested. "Where are you running off to in such a hurry?"

It was a good question. No one was at Daddy's. Despite my hope that he and I might spend more time together now that I was home and set to start at Columbia, it hadn't worked out that way. He had been working as much as ever, and he and my stepmother had left this morning for a long weekend in Vegas. The housekeeper wouldn't even be home, because I'd told her to take a vacation of her own while Daddy was away.

Still, the empty apartment would be better than here. I started pushing against the crush of people around me, trying to figure out where my coat was. Instead of helping me, the girls who had greeted me at the door tried to prevent me from leaving, loudly protesting that I *had* to stay. Voices rose. The music got louder. Someone grabbed my arm.

Screw the coat. I didn't need the coat. The doorman would get me a cab, and I'd be home in ten minutes.

And I was. Except it wasn't really home.

I was shivering when I let myself into the silent, cavernous apartment. I turned on the radio and went rifling through the one suitcase I had yet to unpack, almost frantic. Where was it?

Ah. There. I took a deep, steadying breath.

The countdown started on the radio. I slipped into Art's jacket and listened to the end of 1983.

CHAPTER TWELVE

January 1984

ARTURO

When I walked into my first class, I almost laughed. It was a grad-level class, but everyone was still at least five years younger than I was. And it was so strange to have the tables turned. I was still a campus cop, of course, but now I was a student, too. The experience would probably make me a better cop, but it was still weird.

I say I "almost" laughed, because I wasn't sure if I was capable of laughter anymore. I honestly thought it was possible that Dawn had taken that from me when she hung up on me. After our crushing phone call, I'd turned around and gone back to Boston for the holidays. I couldn't stay in my empty house. I hadn't backed down on my plan to settle permanently in Allenhurst, though. I didn't need Dawn for it to be right. I feared, though, that I *did* need Dawn for...everything else to be right. We'd spent so many years together, and even though we'd only

133

spent a single night *really* together, now that she was gone, there was a hole in my life. I was walking around in a daze, gutted by the fact that I would never bring her coffee between classes again, that when I drove by her building, the light in her window would belong to someone else.

I'd given some serious thought, when I'd gotten on the highway, to turning the car around and heading down to New York instead of up to Boston. But what would I do? Scale her father's building and pound on her window? Physically bar her from attending Columbia?

What could I have said that I hadn't already?

You could have said what you said to the dial tone.

I had this naggy inner voice that wouldn't shut up, that was telling me there was one more thing I hadn't said.

Fuck. All this bravery shit was exhausting.

"Is this seat taken?"

I shifted in my too-small desk toward the voice.

And there she was, the bravest of them all.

Black dress, purple-painted raccoon eyes, puffy blond hair. The sight of her should have been a drink of water for a man dying of thirst, but instead she had the opposite effect. All the moisture in my mouth was gone, and though I was moving my mouth and trying to make sound come out of it, nothing was happening.

She plopped a pink Trapper Keeper on the desk next to mine and sat. "It was too late to apply to the grad psych program here." Then she grinned sheepishly. "Well, too late if you're not having your rich father bribe them to let you in. But I thought I could audit a couple of classes, maybe get a feel for this whole grad-school thing."

"Youth Crime and Justice?" I said, when what I really should have been saying—shouting—was something else entirely.

She shrugged. "Hey, you never know. Maybe I'll go into child psych."

"Dawn?" I got up.

"Yeah?"

"I love you." I grabbed her hand, pulled her to her feet, and lowered my head to kiss her.

Just before my lips hit hers, she grinned and said, "Blah, blah, blah."

ACKNOWLEDGMENTS

My thanks to Gwen Hayes, whose mad editing skills greatly improved this book, and to Polly Watson, whose mad copy editing skills did too.

My pals Audra North and Sandra Owens gave great feedback on early drafts. (A particular shout-out to Audra. I was so stuck that the draft I sent her ended about three-quarters of the way through with "…and then they have sex…and then some more stuff happens, the end. HELP.")

As always, my agent, Courtney Miller-Callihan was full of advice and support and in possession of the enlightened, big-picture view that independent publishing has the potential to float all boats.

Thanks to my friends who answered billions of questions about indie publishing, particularly Zoe York, Melanie Card, and Deborah Cooke.

Dani and Jasmyn at Barclay Publicity did a ton of work on my behalf to make sure this book got into the hands of readers.

I also want to give a shout-out to Elaine Lui, who is

Lainey at laineygossip.com. I've been reading her column for a decade, and it really does do what Dawn eventually tries to do: speak truth to power. Lainey and her writers are smart and funny and wise. They are my source not only for guilty-pleasure celebrity news but for how to think about power, race, and feminism in our contemporary culture. (And I don't know them personally, so this is a totally unbiased plug!)

And of course, the song that inspired this book was "Total Eclipse of the Heart" by Bonnie Tyler. (All the books in this series are inspired by a single song from the 1980s.) I remember taking "mother-daughter slimnastics" (!) at my local YMCA in the 80s, and this song was our "cool down." I'd veg out there on my mat (wearing my black leotard with thin red belt and matching red leg warmers, naturally) next to my mom and absorb what seemed to me then to be its total tragic-ness. I'm glad I could give it a happy ending all these years later.

CONNECT WITH ME

Sign up for my newsletter at jennyholiday.com/newsletter. I send newsletters when I have a new release or a sale, and I sometimes include giveaways and access to freebies only for subscribers. Or you can find me on Twitter at @jenny-holi or Instagram at @holymolyjennyholi. (I'm technically on Facebook, but I'm rarely actually there.) Visit my website at jennyholiday.com.

Reviews really help authors, not only because they help us find new readers but because more reviews means more favorable treatment by retailers' algorithms. If you're moved to leave an honest review of this book or any of my others on the retailer's site where you bought it, I'd be most grateful.

ABOUT THE AUTHOR

Jenny Holiday started writing at age nine when her awesome fourth grade teacher gave her a notebook and told her to start writing some stories. That first batch featured mass murderers on the loose, alien invasions, and hauntings. (Looking back, she's amazed no one sent her to a kid-shrink.) She's been writing ever since. After a detour to get a PhD in geography, she worked as a professional writer for many years. Later, her tastes having evolved from alien invasions to happily-ever-afters, she tried her hand at romance. Today she is a USA Today bestselling author of all sorts of romance novels: contemporary and historical, straight and gay. She lives in London, Ontario.

www.jennyholiday.com
jenny@jennyholiday.com
Twitter: @jennyholi
Instagram: @holymolyjennyholi
Newsletter: jennyholiday.com/newsletter

BOOKS BY JENNY HOLIDAY

NEW WAVE NEWSROOM

The Fixer

The Gossip

The Pacifist

THE FAMOUS SERIES

Famous

Infamous

BRIDESMAIDS BEHAVING BADLY

One and Only

It Takes Two

Merrily Ever After

Three Little Words

THE 49TH FLOOR

Saving the CEO

Sleeping With Her Enemy

The Engagement Game

His Heart's Revenge

REGENCY REFORMERS

The Miss Mirren Mission

The Likelihood of Lucy

Viscountess of Vice

AN EXCERPT FROM THE PACIFIST

NEW WAVE NEWSROOM #3

August 1984

Chapter one

TONY

I wasn't supposed to be taking photographs this semester, but the picture practically composed itself.

It was the tail end of summer, and the courtyard was overripe, teeming with life. Large willow trees poured their lush green waterfalls down toward the lawn, which was studded with purple flowers.

The girl had her back to me, but I knew she was beautiful. There was something about her, her posture maybe, or just her aura, though I normally didn't go in for that kind of hippie shit. She wore a loose, slouchy, mustard-yellow dress belted at the waist with a wide black leather belt, and black ankle boots. She was tall, and her hair added another couple of inches of height, so she blocked my view of the guy she was with.

Still, it was obvious what they were doing. They were locked in a close embrace, and the guy had his arms around her, holding her tight.

Even the animals were transfixed. Well, one of them, anyway. A single squirrel stood a few feet from the amorous couple, head cocked, staring at them, which wasn't necessarily saying much, because the squirrels on this campus were domesticated, fat, and demanding, stalking students who dared to eat outside in Allenhurst College's various quads and courtyards.

There was no doubt in my mind that Beth would run this shot, even though I technically wasn't on the newspaper staff anymore. She might even do it in color, despite the expense. Sometimes the *Allenhurst Examiner*'s first issue of the year—the welcome-back edition—ran a color front page. Getting a shot on the front of the first issue of the year would be a nice way to start what was, depressingly, year five of my degree. It turns out that when you spend more of your time at the newspaper office and partying than you do in class, it catches up with you. Which was why this semester was going to be about classes and nothing else. If I put my head down and worked hard, I could graduate in December. That meant no photography. No parties. No girls. But the idea of one more photo in the paper as a bookend of sorts, a coda to my career as the *Examiner*'s photographer? It had undeniable appeal.

Especially this particular photo.

Another squirrel sauntered over and joined the first, and I had to bite my tongue to keep from laughing. This shot was gonna be so perfect, people were going to think I'd staged it.

It almost felt too easy, inserting myself into this crystalline moment and making it mine. They were standing in the perfect location inside my viewfinder, about two-thirds of the way over from the edge of the ivy-covered building I was planning to use as a framing device. I wouldn't even have to get them to sign release forms, because neither of their faces showed—which was good, because although I wasn't above a little mischief in pursuit of the perfect shot, I didn't relish the idea of interrupting that heated kiss.

I lifted my camera and adjusted the focus. It was going to be an amazing shot, and though I would take the credit for it, it wouldn't be because of me. I was merely lucky enough to stumble onto a perfect scene that had already composed itself.

Click.

Chapter Two

TONY

"Tony, there's someone here to see you."

It was Beth calling through the door of the darkroom, though I had already recognized her knock. Beth was the editor of the *Examiner* and though she was a relentless newshound, she had a surprisingly tentative knock, at least compared to Jenny, her predecessor. Funny that I'd spent so much time in this darkroom over the years that I could distinguish between the knocks of my editors.

I wasn't supposed to be here, working on the second issue of the year. I should have been in my apartment, getting a jump on my reading for the four classes I was taking this semester. I'd never successfully passed four classes in a semester before. If Jenny was still in charge, she would have kicked me out. Beth, who knew all about my self-imposed Semester of No Fun, had not. So, like a junkie in search of a fix, here I was, hunched over in the red-tinged darkness.

Beth's knock was joined by another, more insistent one. More of a pounding, really. Definitely someone else.

The door shook. I moved quickly to shove the photo paper into its black plastic bag, lest my more aggressive visitor knock the door off the hinges and flood the room with light.

"Give me a sec!" Who could want to see me so urgently? My twin sister, Tanya, had graduated, as had Jenny and Dawn and most of my close friends who would know to find me here. That was part of the point. No friends left on campus meant no social temptation and should have made it easier to put my head down and plow through Introduction to Geology. (Yes, I had failed Rocks for Jocks the first time around.)

The pounding continued. "Hang *on!*" I double-checked that my paper was secure in its bag before closing the bag in its box. Then I swung open the door, blinking against the sudden brightness.

Blinking against the sudden beauty.

Because it was her. The girl from the picture. And, all warm medium-brown skin, flashing brown eyes, and scarlet-painted lips, she was gorgeous.

She was also not pleased.

"What the hell is this?" she yelled, waving a copy of Tuesday's paper, which featured her courtyard kiss on the cover. The paper had an Overheard/Overseen on Campus section, and we sometimes ran a photo in it. Beth had, as I'd predicted, moved the feature to the front page and run my shot in color.

"Hey." I flashed my trademark grin that was so

popular with the ladies. Even though I wasn't supposed to be deploying that grin this year, it might mitigate some of the tension rolling off this girl. "It's nice to properly meet you. I'm Tony."

I held out my hand for her to shake, but she looked at it like I was offering her a handful of shit. So I did a lame stretching/fixing-my-hair thing to cover the fact that my overture had been rebuffed, which was stupid, because as pretty as she was, what did I care what this girl thought of me? It was the Semester of No Fun, right?

"Well, Tony," she said, her voice having gone quiet, which was jarring after the yelling. It did something to me, hearing my name on her lips like that, all breathy and intimate. It made me comfortable and uncomfortable at the same time, which made no sense, but there it was. "How about we start with the fact that you have ruined my life."

Okay then. Though she'd turned down the volume, the anger was clearly still there, judging by the way she over-enunciated each syllable and glared at me with her hands on her hips.

"I'm sorry," Beth said. I swung my gaze to my editor. I'd forgotten she was there. "Did he not get you to sign a photo release?"

"I didn't need one," I told her. "No one's face was showing. The subjects can't be identified."

The angry girl let the newspaper flutter to the ground at my feet, dropping it like it was no longer worth the minimal effort required to keep holding it. "The subjects can't be identified?" she echoed, her eyebrows moving up, creating lines in her otherwise smooth forehead. "How many black girls with Afros are there on this campus, do you think?"

Aww, shit. I hadn't thought of it that way. "I don't

know," I said, my mind spinning with the effort of trying to come up with an example of another Afro-sporting girl. But even if I could, her point was valid. Allenhurst was a pretty white place. Still, I wasn't sure what she was so worked up about. It was a great shot. One of my best ever. It would be given a place of pride in my portfolio, assuming I ever got my act together enough to graduate and *need* a portfolio. So, really, why did this girl have her undies in such a bunch? "You looked amazing in the shot, though," I said, deploying some flattery to bolster my case. "That dress was totally rad, and there was something about the way you were holding yourself, your posture, that was really compelling."

"My posture," she said, her nose wrinkling like she'd smelled something gross. "My posture was compelling. That's all you have to say?"

"What do you want me to say? You can't retract a photo."

"I want you to say, 'I'm sorry I ruined your life.' I want you to understand that you can't just walk around invading people's private moments without creating consequences for them."

Whoa. I held up my hands like she was robbing me. Melodramatic much?

She rolled her eyes, but really quickly and really subtly, so much so that I almost missed it. Most people would have, but I had trained myself to see things other people didn't. And for some reason, that low-key eye roll made me angrier than a more overt one would have. It was like I was so incredibly far beneath her that it wasn't even worth her time for her to properly communicate that sentiment to me.

Then she turned and started walking away.

So this girl nearly broke down my darkroom door and now she was *dismissing* me?

Yeah, no, not so much.

I let the jet of anger that erupted in my chest propel me after her. "Wait!" I shouted, ignoring Beth's attempts to call me back. The angry girl kept walking briskly. I followed her out of the warren that was the *Examiner's* basement newsroom. "Hang on!" I said, as she mounted the stairs that would take her back to the ground floor of the building. She ignored me. It was like I wasn't even there, and god*damn*, that made me mad. "So you just came to shake your finger at me and now you're not even going to speak to me?" I called as I finally caught up with her, trying not to pant.

That stopped her. She turned and paused, poised in the doorway, one foot inside the building, the other out. "What's left to say, Tony? You were actually right: you *can't* retract a photo."

Two things about what she said pissed me off. The first was that she knew my name, and I still didn't know hers. She had barged onto *my* turf. Why should she have the upper hand? The second was the way she said "can't," stressing it ever so slightly, like it was such a shock that someone as simple as I could be right about something. Her words were sharp little sticks poking at my gut.

"What's your name?" I asked. The question came out sounding mean, which I hadn't necessarily intended, but that was okay, because something about this girl had me spoiling for a fight.

"Why? So the next time you intrude on a private moment and plaster it all over the newspaper, you can add my name to the caption?" One side of her scarlet-painted upper lip curled, a little proto-sneer. Like with the eye roll,

I was annoyed that I apparently wasn't worthy of a full-blown sneer.

"I'm not sure how you can say that was a private moment," I shot back. "If you wanted it to be private, maybe you shouldn't have been doing it, oh, I don't know, *in public.*"

She surprised me then by sighing. Those lips I'd been staring at so intently fell open to make room for the long, resigned exhalation. That sigh confused me, because it felt like a defeated sigh, but surely that couldn't be right? I couldn't have won that easily? It also immediately brought to mind other circumstances in which lips could part on a sigh like that, but I shoved that thought right back down where it came from. The semester had barely even started, and no way was I so hard up that I was going to let myself perv on this prickly, unreasonable chick, no matter how gorgeous she was.

Then her eyes slipped closed and her shoulders slumped, confirming my initial sense that the fight had left her. That something had shifted between us. When she opened her eyes, her gaze held mine for a long moment before she turned again to leave.

If she had surprised me with that sigh, with how easily she'd given up the fight just then, I downright *shocked* myself by reaching my hand out, just before she escaped, and resting it on her arm. I wasn't exerting any pressure, but it was enough to stop her. "Tell me about these consequences," I said. But even as I posed the question, I asked myself why? Why did I care? I didn't owe this girl anything. All I had done was take a photo of her in a public place. Still, I needed to know. "Tell me about the consequences you mentioned." I tried not to think about how I was touching her bare skin, about how incredibly soft it was.

As if she'd heard the very thoughts I was trying not to have, she dropped her gaze to my hand on her arm. My own gaze followed, and I noticed for the first time that she was wearing a Siouxsie and the Banshees T-shirt. I added that fact to pile of surprises that had accumulated over the past few minutes. I loved that band. I wanted to tell her, but it was the wrong thing to say.

And then the touch seemed wrong, too. It was just my hand on her arm, and she hadn't objected or moved to escape it, but it was suddenly intrusive, too intimate—like the picture? Shit. Had she been right about that?

Maybe it was just that it was too much to adjust to, this moment of peace, of human contact, after our adversarial introduction. Too whiplash-inducing.

"I should not have been kissing that guy," she said, still looking at my hand.

"He wasn't identifiable." I'm not sure if I intended to reassure her or to defend myself. Regardless, from my angle, she'd been completely obscuring her paramour in the shot. All you could see of him were his arms wrapped around her, and he hadn't been wearing a watch or anything else that might have given him away. "You couldn't tell who he was."

"Yes," she said, finally lifting her gaze and looking me in the eye. "But you could tell who he *wasn't*." Then she shook my hand off her arm and jogged down the steps that ran from the door to the sidewalk. I'd been dismissed. Again.

I *really* didn't like being dismissed by this girl, apparently. "Hey!" I called after her, loud enough for her to stop at the bottom of the steps and shoot me a skeptical look, like she was a mature-beyond-her-years person tolerating the whim of a child. "Tell me your name."

"My name is…" She paused long enough that I suspected she was making something up, giving me a fake name. "My name is Laraline."

LARALINE

So far, the Semester of Fun was not turning out to be very much fun.

I mean, kissing Brian had been fun, but certainly not enough that it had been worth the trouble it had caused… and had yet to cause. I still had dinner with my parents to get through on Friday.

I let myself into my apartment and blew out a breath. Wow, that Tony guy had rattled me. I don't know what I had expected. That he would be contrite, I guess. It hadn't occurred to me that the person who took such an amazing picture—and it *had* been amazing—would be capable of being such a shithead.

"Dove? Hey!"

My roommate, Cynthia, emerged from the kitchen into the small entryway of our apartment, wiping her hands on her apron.

"My name is Laraline," I said, for the second time today.

"Right," she said. "Sorry. I keep forgetting."

I was in the process of trying to shed my nickname, Dove. The peacemaker. *Laraline* was Latin for "seagull," and at some point early in my undergrad career, my friends had decided that I was misnamed. If I was going to be a bird, they said, I should be the bird of peace, since I spent as much time keeping the peace in my family as I did studying. My campaign of appeasement had begun ten years ago when my sister, Phoebe, got sick, and it had intensified when she died. It was like since the transplant didn't work, I had moved into overcompensation mode, constantly trying to make things okay, even though the rational part of my brain knew that was impossible.

So: Dove. It started as a joke, and then it just kind of...stuck. No more, though. It was the Semester of Fun, so I'd forced Dove to fly south.

But if you had to explicitly label a thing—it's the Semester of Fun!—and keep reminding yourself of the existence of that thing, it probably meant that thing wasn't going to come naturally to you.

Which is another way of saying that the Semester of Fun had been Jason's idea.

Not that label, and not necessarily my interpretation of it, which was that I was going to go out there and kiss a bunch of other boys. I had a feeling he wouldn't like that part. Like a lot of men, Jason was blind to his own double standards. He was my father's protégé in more ways than one.

He'd sat me down on his last visit, just before school started, and said that he would be back at Christmas and would want to "talk seriously" to me then, but that we shouldn't be "exclusive" for this "last little stretch," you know, "just to make sure." We'd been together so long, we should experience the world without each other for a few months, he'd said.

I was surprised by how much he'd hurt my feelings. I'd long since resigned myself to the fact that Jason wasn't going to be the great love of my life in the style of the movies. We would never kiss in the rain or fight duels to defend each other's honor. I wasn't even convinced that kind of love existed. But I liked Jason a lot. He understood the way things were in my family, and that wasn't nothing.

And there was so much invested in the idea of Jason and me.

So when he'd gotten on that plane to go back to Greece, leaving me hollowed out by betrayal, I'd decided hell, maybe he had a point. I didn't *feel* like he had a point, but my rational mind, the part that was apparently in charge of my pride, forced me to have a "what's good for the goose is good for the gander" response.

And though it had begun with me merely going through the motions, I had started to actually…have fun. At least until that photo ran in the paper. Flirting was fun. Kissing was fun. As the first week of my last year of grad school unfolded, I started to *really* feel it. It was dawning on me that this semester was really it. My last chance to do what I wanted every day.

My last chance to be my own person.

My last chance to…live.

Maybe Jason had been onto something.

"You had some calls." Cynthia pulled me out of my thoughts and into a quick, hard half-hug. "Come into the kitchen. I'm making cookies for work. I need a tester."

"I'm sorry I jumped down your throat with the name thing." A rush of affection for my best friend inspired me to grab her and give her a proper, full-on hug. We'd been assigned as roommates five years ago, our freshman year. The dormitory gods had been smiling on me the day they hitched me to the wide-eyed farm girl from Iowa. I hadn't thought so at the time, because we seemed to have nothing in common. She was a blue-eyed, blond-haired daughter of corn farmers, at Allenhurst on a scholarship and majoring in civil engineering. I was a black girl from Boston's Beacon Hill, majoring in art history, and I was a legacy at the school. Not only had my father attended, he was a famous professor in the classics department. As a faculty kid, I received free tuition, even though we had more than enough to cover it. Once Cynthia and I got over the shock of our differences and discovered that your sameness with another person could be much bigger than your difference, I had often wished that I could somehow transfer my tuition waiver to her.

"It's okay," she said, pulling away but keeping hold of my hand and leading me into the kitchen.

"What kind this time?" I asked, inhaling the heavenly smell of caramelized sugar.

"Chocolate chip with crunched-up potato chips."

I laughed but snagged one, knowing the weird combo would be amazing. Maybe it was the engineer in her, but Cynthia loved tinkering in the kitchen, and coming up with cookie creations that were as delicious as they were unlikely was one of her trademarks.

"Oh my God," I said through a mouthful of the sweet-salty goodness. "The jerks at work don't deserve these. Can I bring some to the rally tomorrow night?"

"Oh, right, that's tomorrow! Yes, of course." She started rummaging in a cupboard for a cookie tin. "Let's take them all. Much better cause than Rogers and Steenburger." Cynthia worked in an administrative capacity at a small engineering firm in the next town over. She had hoped it would be a foot in the door to an actual engineering job. It irritated the hell out of me that a year and a half later, she was still answering the phones and doing grunt-work to support the guys who worked there.

And making them cookies. Which was why I was

always trying to steal them. Rogers and Steenburger and their minions didn't deserve her cookies.

Cynthia went to the phone mounted on the wall and picked up a piece of notepaper she'd tacked to the bulletin board beneath it. "So, your mom called twice, once at five and again at five-thirty. She wants you to call her back before eight."

Which translated into: she wanted me to call her back before my father got home. "I'm seeing them tomorrow night, but I suspect she wants to 'strategize' on how to handle my father after Photogate."

Which translated into: after a speech about how shocked and disappointed she was, she would feed me the lines that would placate my father. Because that's how we rolled in our family, post-Phoebe.

I had hoped against hope that my father wouldn't see Tuesday's newspaper. That he'd be busy getting the new semester off the ground. In addition to his usual undergrads, he had two new doctoral students starting this fall —people came from all over the world to work with my dad because he was the world's foremost expert on the architecture of ancient Greece.

But no. Tuesday evening he had made a rare appearance at my apartment. Though he would often pick me up outside when I was heading home for a visit, he hadn't been upstairs since the day Cynthia and I moved in four years ago.

To say he'd been angry was an understatement. He didn't blow up, though, which was actually worse than if he had. He'd merely informed me that he'd be picking me up Friday at five and taking me back to Boston for dinner.

"Annnndd," Cynthia drawled, hugging the notepaper to her chest, "you had *one* more message."

"Who was it?" I asked, wondering why she was being so coy.

"Brian."

Aww, crap. See? This was why the Semester of Fun was not all it was cracked up to be. Brian had been nice enough. He was an art history undergrad, and he was cute. We'd been at a guest lecture on Cubism and had gotten into a bit of a debate afterward. When he'd asked me to go for a drink, I'd thought, *Well, what the hell? Semester of Fun, right?*

"Who's Brian?" Cynthia asked. "Is he the guy you were kissing in that picture?" She had seen the picture, of course—the whole campus had seen the picture—but I'd been steadfast in my refusal to discuss it with her, which wasn't typical. Usually we talked everything to death.

"He's no one."

"No one who called here and, when I told him you weren't home, asked me what your favorite kind of flower was?" she prodded, eyebrows raised. "He *was* the picture guy!"

I sighed. I really, really didn't want Brian to become a thing. He was supposed to have been a kiss, and that was it.

Cynthia tried to hand me the notepaper, but I waved her off. "I'm not calling him back." I moved to take a cookie from the cooling rack, but she pivoted and blocked me.

"But who *is* he?"

"You know what Jason said before he left," I protested, hating that I was suddenly on the defensive. "I wasn't doing anything wrong."

She didn't speak right away, just stared at me with her eyes narrowed for what felt like an hour. Then she finally said, "Listen." She was speaking in her Engineer Voice, the one she used when she was really applying herself to a problem. "I don't care about Jason. I've never said this to you in so many words, but I'm going to say it now: You don't have to marry Jason."

Her words were a slap to the face. I actually reared back a little, physically. But when I opened my mouth to protest that yes, I did have to marry Jason, that I even *wanted* to marry Jason, or at least I *didn't mind* marrying Jason, all things considered, she presented me with her palm.

But then, inexplicably, she lightened up and flashed me a smile. "I also don't care if you dropped trou on the quad and participated in an orgy. I just want to know who this Brian guy is! You've been dating Jason the entire time I've known you, and suddenly here's this other guy? Come on! Give me something!"

I laughed, partly because the exaggerated faces she was making were funny, but partly because of the weird emotional roller coaster I'd been on today, and gave up my stonewalling. "He's just this art history kid—a sophomore. He isn't a big deal. Honestly. If he was a big deal, I would tell you."

"A younger man. About time." She was referring to the fact that Jason was five years older than I was. She handed me a cookie.

What was I going to do next year when I didn't have Cynthia around to make cookies for me? Well, that and coax out all my secrets? The prospect of Cynthia just...not being there made my throat tighten.

"Hey," I said, suddenly thinking that the Semester of Fun didn't just have to be about boys. "A band I'm kind of interested in is playing at the A-Hole tonight. You want to check them out?" Since I'd started grad school and Cynthia had started working full-time, we didn't hang out the way we used to. Of course, we saw each other all the time in the apartment, but a show on a "school night" wasn't something we would generally do these days.

My roommate grinned. "I sure do."

BRIDESMAIDS BEHAVING BADLY #2

CHAPTER ONE

TUESDAY—ELEVEN DAYS BEFORE THE WEDDING

Jane! I thought you were *never* going to get here!"

"I came as quickly as I could," Jane said, trying to keep the annoyance out of her tone as she allowed herself to be herded into her friend Elise's house. She exchanged resigned smiles with her fellow bridesmaids—the ones who had obviously taken Elise's "Emergency bridesmaids meeting at my house NOW!" text more seriously than Jane had.

Gia and Wendy were sprawled on Elise's couch, braiding some kind of dried grass–type thing. Wendy, Jane's best friend, blew her a kiss.

Jane tried to perform her traditional catching of Wendy's kiss—it was their thing, dating back to childhood —but Elise thrust a mug of tea into Jane's hand before it could close over the imaginary kiss. Earlier that summer,

Elise had embraced and then discarded a plan to start her wedding reception with some kind of complicated cocktail involving tea, and as a result, Jane feared she and the girls were doomed to a lifetime of Earl Grey. Their beloved bridezilla had thought nothing of special ordering twenty-seven unreturnable boxes of premium English tea leaves. She also apparently thought nothing of forcing her friends to endure the rejected reception beverage again and again. And again.

"Jane's here, so now you can tell us about the big emergency," Gia said. "And whatever it is, I'm sure she'll figure out a solution." She smiled at Jane. "You're so . . . smart."

Jane had a feeling that *smart* wasn't the word Gia initially meant to use. The girls—well, Gia and Elise, anyway—were always telling Jane to loosen up. But they also relied on her to solve their problems. They liked having it both ways. She was the den mother, but they were forever teasing her about being too rigid. Which was kind of rich, lately, coming from Elise, who had turned into a matrimonial drill sergeant. Jane put up with it because she loved them. Besides, *somebody* had to be the responsible one.

"Well," Jane teased, "this had better be a capital-E emergency because I was in the middle of having my costume for Toronto Comicon fitted when you texted." She opened the calf-length trench coat she'd thrown over her costume at the seamstress's when Elise's text arrived. It was the kind of coat women wore when seducing their boyfriends—or so she assumed, not having personally attempted to seduce anyone since Felix. She should probably just get rid of the coat because there were likely no seductions in her future, either.

"Hello!" Gia exclaimed. "*What* is that?"

"Xena: Warrior Princess," Wendy answered before Jane could.

"I have no idea what that means, but you look hot," Gia said.

Jane did a little twirl. The costume was really coming together. The seamstress had done a kick-ass job with the leather dress, armor, and arm bands, and all Jane needed to do was figure out something for Xena's signature weapon and she'd be set. "It was a cult TV show from the 1990s,"she explained. Gia was a bit younger than the rest of them. But who was Jane kidding? The real reason Gia didn't know about Xena was that she was a Cool Girl. As a model—an honest-to-goodness, catwalk-strutting, appearing-in-Calvin-Klein-ads model—she was too busy with her fabulous life to have time to watch syndicated late-night TV. "It's set in a sort of alternative ancient Greece, but it's leavened with other mythologies . . . " She trailed off because the explanation sounded lame even to her fantasy-novelist, geek-girl ears.

"Xena basically goes around kicking ass, and then she and her sidekick get it on with some lesbian action," Wendy said, summing things up in her characteristically concise way.

"Really?" Gia narrowed her eyes at Jane. "Is there something you're trying to tell us?"

"No!" Jane protested.

"Because you haven't had a boyfriend since Felix," Gia went on. "And you guys broke up, what? Four years ago?"

"Five," Wendy said.

It was true. But what her friends refused to accept was that she was single by choice. She had made a sincere effort, with Felix, whom she'd met halfway through university and stayed with until she was twenty-six, to enter the world of love and relationships that everyone was always insisting was so important. Felix had taught her many things, foremost among them that she was better off alone.

You know we'll love you no matter what," Gia said. "Who you sleep with doesn't make a whit of difference."

"I'm not gay, Gia! I just admire Xena. She didn't need men to get shit done. We could all—"

A very loud episode of throat clearing from Elise interrupted Jane's speech on the merits of independence, whether you were a pseudo-Greek warrior princess or a modern girl trying to get along in the world.

"Sorry." Jane sometimes forgot that most people did not share her views of love and relationships.

"I'm sure this is all super interesting, you guys?" Elise said. "But we have a serious problem on our hands?" She was talking fast and ending declarative statements with question marks—sure signs she was stressed. Elise always sounded like an auctioneer on uppers when she was upset.

"I need to grab my phone because I'm expecting the cake people to call? So sit down and brace yourselves and I'll be right back?"

Jane sank into a chair and warily eyed a basket of spools of those brown string-like ribbon things—the kind that were always showing up tied around Mason jars of layered salads on Pinterest. She wasn't really sure how or why Elise had decided not to outsource this stuff like normal people did when they got married. The whole wedding had become a DIY-fest. "What are we doing with this stuff?" she asked the others.

"No idea," said Wendy, performing a little eye roll. "I'm just doing what I'm told."

Jane grinned. Although she, Wendy, Gia, and Elise were a tightly knit foursome, they also sorted into pairs of best friends: Jane and Wendy had grown up together and had met Elise during freshman orientation at university. They'd picked up Gia when they were seniors and Gia was a freshman—Elise had been her resident assistant—RA— and the pair had become fast friends despite the age difference.

"We are weaving table runners out of raffia ribbon," Gia said. She dropped her strands and reached for her purse. "Slide that tea over here—quick, before she gets back."

"God bless you," Jane said when Gia pulled a flask of whiskey out of her purse and tipped some into Jane's mug. If the "emergency" that had pulled Jane away from her cosplay fitting—not to mention a planned evening of writing—was going to involve table runners, she was going to need something to dull the edges a bit.

Elise reappeared. Jane practiced her nonchalant face as she sipped her "tea" and tried not to cough. She wasn't normally much of a drinker, but desperate times and all that.

"I didn't want to repeat myself, so I've been holding out on Gia and Wendy?" Elise said. "But there's been a . . . disruption to the wedding plans?"

I love you, but God help me, those are declarative sentences. Sometimes Jane had trouble turning off her inner editor. Job hazard.

"Oh my God, are you leaving Jay?" Wendy asked.

"Why would you say that?" Elise turned to Wendy in bewilderment.

Now, that was a legitimate question, the inner editor said—at least in the sense that it was meant to end with a question mark. The actual content of Wendy's question was kind of insensitive. But Wendy had trouble with change, and Elise pairing off and doing the whole till-death-do-us-part

thing? That was some major change for their little friend group. Jane might have had trouble with it, too, except it was plainly obvious to anyone with eyeballs that Elise was head-over-heels, one hundred percent gaga for her fiancé.

"I'm kidding!" Wendy said, a little too vehemently. Elise looked like she might have to call for smelling salts.

"Take a breath," Gia said to Elise, "and tell us what's wrong."

Elise did as instructed, then flopped into a chair. "Jay's brother is coming to the wedding."

"Jay has a brother?" Jane asked. Though she was guilty of maybe not paying one hundred percent attention to every single wedding-related detail—for example, she'd recused herself from the debate over the merits of sage green versus grass green for the ribbons that would adorn the welcome bags left in the guests' hotel rooms—she was pretty sure she had a handle on all the major players.

"His name is Cameron MacKinnon."

That didn't clear things up. "Jay Smith has a brother named Cameron MacKinnon?" she asked. Was that even possible?

"Half brother," Elise said. "You know how Jay's mom is single?" It was true. There had been no "father of the groom" in Elise's carefully drafted program. "Well, she split from Jay's dad when Jay was nine. Then a couple years later, she had a brief relationship with another man. Cameron is the product of that—that's why his last name is MacKinnon and Jay's is Smith."

"But he wasn't always going to come to the wedding?" Gia asked. "Were they estranged?"

"They're not particularly close. There are eleven years between them—Cameron was in first grade when Jay left for school—but they're not estranged," Elise said. "He wasn't going to be able to make it to the wedding because he was supposed to be in Iraq. He was in the army. But now he's . . . not."

"That sounds ominous," Wendy said.

"Look, here's the thing," Elise said, sitting up straight, her voice suddenly and uncharacteristically commanding. "Cameron is a problem. He's wild. He drives too fast, drinks too much, sleeps around. You name it—if it's sketchy, he's into it."

"And this is *Jay's* brother," Jane said. Because no offense, she liked Jay fine, but Jay was. . . a tad under-whelming. He was an accountant. No matter what they were doing—football game, barbecue, hiking—he dressed in dark jeans and a polo shirt, like it was casual Friday at the office. To be honest, Jane had never really been sure what Elise saw in him. The girls were always telling *her* to loosen up, but compared to Jay, she was the life of the party.

"Yes," Elise said. "Cameron is Jay's brother, and he must be stopped."

"Dun, dun, dun!" Wendy mock-sang.

"Hey, I can totally switch gears and weave this thing into a noose," Gia said, holding up a lopsided raffia braid.

"I'm not kidding."

Elise's tone made everyone stop laughing and look up. The upspeak was gone, and the bride had become a warrior, eyes narrowed, lips pursed. "He's a high school dropout. He burned down a barn outside Thunder Bay when he was seventeen. He was charged with arson, the whole deal. Jay says his mother still hasn't lived it down. And there's talk he got a girl pregnant in high school."

"What happened?" asked a rapt Gia.

Elise shrugged. "Her family moved out of town, so no one really knows."

"Wow," Wendy said, echoing Jane's thoughts. Jane had initially assumed Elise was being melodramatic about this black-sheep brother—as she was about nearly every-thing wedding related—but this guy *did* sound like bad news.

"Anyway." Elise brandished an iPad in front of her like it was a weapon. "Cameron MacKinnon is *not* ruining my wedding. And if he's left to his own devices, he will. From what Jay says, he won't be able to help it." She poked at the iPad. "This changes everything. We need to redo the schedule—and the job list."

The words *job list* practically gave Jane hives. Elise had turned into a total bridezilla, but by unspoken agreement, the bridesmaids had been going along with whatever she wanted. It was the path of least resistance. But also, they truly wanted Elise to have the wedding of her dreams. Even if it was painful for everyone else.

But, oh, the *job list*. The job list was like the Hydra, a serpentine monster you could never get on top of. You crossed off a job, and two more sprouted to take its place. Jane had already hand-stenciled three hundred invitations, planned and executed two showers, joined Pinterest as instructed for the express purpose of searching out "home-made bunting," tried on no fewer than twenty-three dresses—all purple—and this Cameron thing aside, it looked like today was going to be spent weaving table runners. And they still had the bachelorette party and the rehearsal dinner to get through, never mind the main event.

It boggled the mind. Elise was an interior designer, so of course she cared how things looked, but even so, Jane was continuously surprised at how much the wedding was preoccupying her friend. She could only hope they would get their funny, creative, sweet friend back after it was all over.

"Cameron is coming to town tomorrow," Elise said. "I don't know why he couldn't just arrive a day ahead of the wedding like the rest of the out-of-town guests, but it is what it is." She let the iPad clatter onto the coffee table. "I don't even know how to add this to the job list, but somehow, we have to babysit Cameron for the next week and a half."

"We?" Wendy echoed.

"Yes. He needs to be supervised at all times until the wedding—until after the post-wedding breakfast, actually. Then he can wreak whatever havoc he wants."

"Hang on," Jane said. "I agree that he sounds like bad news. But let's say, for the sake of argument, he did something horrible and got arrested tomorrow. I don't really see how that would have an impact on your wedding at all, because—"

Elise looked up, either ignoring or legitimately not hearing Jane. "You can't do it, Gia. You're my maid of honor, and I need you at my side at all times."

"Sure thing," Gia said.

Easy for her to say. Gia had purposely not taken any modeling jobs the two weeks before the wedding. She had plenty of time to lounge around braiding dried foliage and looking effortlessly beautiful in sweatpants. Also, there was the part where she was a millionaire.

Elise started scrolling through some kind of calendar app on her iPad. "Now, tomorrow we're supposed to be spraypainting the tea sets gold."

Jane looked around. *Spray-painting the tea sets gold?* Why was no one else confused by that sentence?

"But we'll have to do that in the afternoon," Elise went on, "because—"

"I have to work tomorrow," Wendy said. And when Elise looked up blankly, she added, "Tomorrow is Wednesday."

Jane was about to protest that she had to work tomorrow, too. Book seven of the Clouded Cave series wasn't going to write itself. Just because she didn't have to be in court like Wendy didn't mean her job wasn't important. She had an inbox full of fan mail from readers clamoring for the next book, not to mention a contractual deadline that got closer every day.

Elise continued, seemingly oblivious to her friends' weekday employment obligations. "Tomorrow we also need to do a practice run of boutonniere, corsage, and bouquet making. I finagled a vendor pass to the commercial fruit and flower market, but we need to get there early. So we should do the flowers in the morning and paint the tea sets in the afternoon. We'll meet in Mississauga at five thirty, but someone needs to pick up Cameron and make sure he behaves all day."

"I'll do it," said Jane, mentally calculating that to be at the suburban flower market by five thirty, she'd have to get up at four a.m. Also, there was the part about spending the afternoon spray-painting tea sets. It didn't take a genius to figure out which was the lesser of the two proverbial evils. She could babysit this Cameron dude. She'd treat him like a character in one of her books—

figure him out, then make him do her bidding. "Give me the wild man's flight info, and I'll pick him up."

"I thought it would be best if you did it," Elise said, still scrolling and tapping like a maniac. "I mean, your job is so—"

Wait for it.

"Flexible."

But at least she hadn't said anything about—

"And you're so responsible. I feel like this is your kind of task."

Jane stifled a sigh. Everyone always called her responsible, but they made it sound so . . . boring. She preferred to think of herself as conscientious.

"I really, really appreciate this, Jane," Elise said, finally looking up from her iPad and gracing Jane with a smile so wide and sincere that it almost made her breath catch.

Yes. Right. That was why she was voluntarily submitting to this bridesmaid torture-gig. Her friend Elise was still somewhere inside the bridezilla that was currently manning the controls, and she was so, so happy to be marrying the love of her life. That was the important thing. It made even Jane's heart, which was usually immune to these kinds of sentiments, twist a little. A wedding wasn't in her future, and she was fine with that, but all of this planning made her think of her parents' wedding pictures, the pair of them all decked out in their shaggy 1970s glory. Had they been in love like Elise and Jay, before the accident? Maybe at the start, but probably not for long, given her father's addiction. He was never violent, but he wasn't very . . . lovable.

But now was not the time for a pity party, so she smiled back at Elise. "No problem."

"You need to meet his plane, take him to Jay's, and

make sure he doesn't do anything crazy. Jay will be home as soon as he can after work, and then you can leave for the evening and we'll figure out the rest of the schedule from there."

"Got it."

Elise reached out and squeezed her hand. "Seriously. Making sure Cameron doesn't ruin my wedding is the best present you could give me."

She waved away Elise's thanks. This was going to be a piece of cake. Or at least better than tea set spray-painting duty. After all, how bad could this Cameron MacKinnon guy be?

www.ingramcontent.com/pod-product-compliance
Lightning Source LLC
Chambersburg PA
CBHW050942120626
46552CB00001B/341